# Champagne and Catastrophes

### A
## Peridale Cafe
### MYSTERY

# AGATHA FROST

First published in print October 23rd 2018

For questions and comments about this book, please contact
pinktreepublishing@gmail.com

www.pinktreepublishing.com
www.agathafrost.com

ISBN: 9781729125885
Imprint: Independently published

# A Peridale Cafe MYSTERY

Book Fourteen

# 1

"You're breaking up," Julia said as the video of her daughter jittered across her phone's screen. *"Jessie?"*

"M-M-*trailia*-g-d-" Jessie's fragmented voice struggled through the tiny speakers and the bad connection. "It's awesome!"

"I think she's trying to say, 'Australia is awesome.'" Barker's shout from the dining room made Julia jump. "Ask her what she's been up to."

"I would if this silly thing worked!" Julia jabbed the screen with her finger, but the video of Jessie had devolved into a mushy mess of pixels. "I just want to check that our daughter is alive and well. Is that too much to ask?" Julia shook the phone and squinted at the screen. "*Jessie*? Can you hear me?"

"Try the garden," Barker called over the sound of his typing. "Sometimes, the signal is better out there."

Still in her dressing gown and slippers, Julia unlocked the cottage's front door and hurried into the garden, her eyes fixed on the phone. As though a magic spell had been cast, Jessie's face snapped into focus.

"There you are!" Julia cried, her smile beaming. "I'd almost forgotten what you looked like."

"I've only been gone for six days," Jessie said with a signature eye roll. "Are you in your dressing gown?"

"You *are* nine hours ahead." Julia pulled her pink gown together as she peered up and down the quiet lane—not that she had any close neighbours to catch her outside in her nightclothes. "It's only eight in the morning here. What have you done today? Tell me everything."

"Hello, Miss S!" Billy called. His face appeared behind Jessie on the tiny screen. "We're missing your cakes."

"Shove off, Billy." Jessie pushed him away from the camera's view. "Everything is fine. You're not worrying, are you?"

Julia considered her response as she paced across the grass. When Jessie had mentioned that she wanted to spend a month backpacking around Australia, Julia had been apprehensive. When she had realised Jessie was telling her and not asking, Julia had been even more anxious. Though Jessie was eighteen and legally an adult, Julia couldn't help but worry. It soothed her a little to know that Jessie's boyfriend, Billy, and her older brother, Alfie, were there with her, but it hadn't stopped Julia from losing sleep.

"*Mum?* Is everything okay?"

"Oh, yes." Julia nodded and pushed a smile onto her lips. "I haven't been worrying."

"You know I can see you, right?" Jessie rolled her eyes again. "You're a terrible liar. There's no need to worry. We're having a great time, and I've got Alfie here. He's travelled the world twice over."

Jessie tapped something on her screen, and the camera suddenly flipped to show Alfie and Billy sitting around a campfire as a pink sun faded into the orange sky behind them.

"You know what I'm like," Julia said with a wave of

her hand. "Don't worry about me worrying. That will make me worry more. I don't think I'm making much sense, am I?"

"You're not." Jessie chuckled. "But you *are* crazy. How's the café? How's Mowgli?"

"Everything is fine here. Tell me about *your* day! Don't skip the details."

Jessie explained how they had hitched a ride in the back of a 'very cool guy's truck' to a popular backpacking hostel fifty miles outside Sydney, where they were sharing dorms with thirty other 'really cool' people. Julia listened carefully, smiling and nodding, hoping her distress was not written all over her face.

"We're going horse riding tomorrow." Jessie let out a long yawn. "One of the guys here knows someone who knows a guy who runs a farm. Should be fun."

"Just be safe." Julia's voice faltered. "I miss you."

"Six days, cake lady."

"I'm allowed to miss you."

Jessie looked around before bringing the phone closer to her face and saying, "I miss you too, but only a little bit. Just don't freak out, okay? I'm going to have a beer with the guys. Love you."

"Love you too," Julia said loudly. "And don't drink too—"

Jessie ended the call before Julia could finish her warning. Julia dropped onto the creaky, moss-covered bench under her sitting room window and let out a deep sigh as she peered up at the bright blue, August-morning sky. Though she had no idea how the next twenty-four days were going to go, Julia was sure the ache in her chest was only going to grow with each passing day.

Julia had no idea how long she had been sitting on the bench thinking about Jessie, but a car driving slowly down the lane dragged her out of her daydream. She watched as it ground to a halt in front of the only other cottage Julia could see from her garden. She stood and pulled her gown tight as she watched a tall, slender woman with pin-straight, sandy-coloured hair climb out. The mystery woman peered over the top of her car at the tiny cottage, shielding her eyes from the sun.

"A new neighbour?" Julia's question drifted on the warm morning breeze as she dipped down behind the bushes circling her garden.

She squinted over the edge of the greenery for a better look, but under the sun's glare, the newcomer was nothing more than a head of gleaming hair. She walked around her car and popped open the boot before pulling out a large cardboard box.

After hurrying inside, Julia swiftly changed out of her dressing gown and into a peach-coloured summer dress. She ran a brush through her chocolatey curls, spritzed on a little sweet perfume, and threw on a coat of black mascara.

"*New neighbour!*" Julia called into the dining room as she ran towards the kitchen. "We have a new neighbour!"

"*Huh?*" Barker replied, his fingers still drumming on the keyboard. "How's Jessie?"

"She's fine." Julia peered into the packed fridge until her eyes landed on the orange-zest carrot cake she had baked the previous night. "Someone is moving into Emily Burns' old cottage."

"That's been empty for a year."

"*Exactly!*" Julia pulled the cake from the fridge and peeled the lid from its plastic display case before transferring it onto one of her prettiest china plates. "I'm going to introduce myself. Why don't you come?"

"Deadline," he replied, his typing only pausing so he could slurp his coffee. "Maybe later."

Julia headed to the front door, cake in hand, before realising her new neighbour wouldn't have any tea or coffee making ingredients yet. Doubling back, she filled a plastic carrier bag with half a jar of coffee, a box of black tea bags, a bag of sugar, and a small carton of milk. She almost closed the bag but threw in a handful of individually-wrapped peppermint and liquorice tea, just in case the new neighbour liked Julia's favourite tea. With excitement fluttering in her chest, Julia left her cottage.

Making her way down the garden path, Julia wondered if she was being a little premature in welcoming her new neighbour to the village. The newcomer might want to be left alone to unpack, after all—though Julia knew nobody would turn down a freshly baked cake; nobody nice, at least. Shaking these thoughts from her mind, she remembered that Emily Burns had appeared to greet Julia the second her moving van had pulled up outside her cottage three years ago. If she sensed hostility from the new arrival, she would hand over the cake and leave her to her day.

Julia lingered by the gate and peered through the open cottage door. While she waited for her new neighbour to appear, she assessed what had once been Emily's beautiful and prized rose garden. Weeds had taken over the grass, which had yellowed thanks to the recent drought. Even though vibrant red roses had persevered without attendance, they lacked the refinement that Emily's daily pruning had brought.

The new neighbour walked out of the cottage, dusting her hands. She made it halfway down the garden path before she noticed Julia and stopped in her tracks.

"Oh, hello," the woman said, her brows knitting. "Wait. *Julia?* Julia South?"

Julia stared at the woman who knew her name, but it only took her a second to realise she was staring not at a stranger but someone she had once called a close friend.

*"Leah?* Leah Burns!"

"Now, there's a blast from the past." Leah's hands drifted up to her mouth as a grin spread across her face. "I've been back in Peridale for five minutes, and Julia South has turned up on my doorstep with a cake! If I didn't know better, I'd think I was dreaming. Look at you! You haven't aged a day."

"Neither have you." Julia stared at her old friend in disbelief. "I can't believe you're my new neighbour. How long has it been? It must be twenty years!"

"Twenty-one years exactly," Leah said as she looked around at the green countryside surrounding them. "I haven't stepped foot in Peridale since 1997, and this place hasn't changed one bit. What are you doing here? Nobody knew I was coming."

"I live across the lane." Julia nodded to her cottage. "I saw your car pull up and I thought I'd welcome you."

"You're telling me I would have got one of your delicious cakes even if you didn't know me?" Leah shook her head in disbelief. "You really haven't changed. I still dream about your chocolate fudge brownies. I can't imagine how much better they are now that you've had twenty years practise."

"I run a small café in the village," Julia said. "What are you doing here?"

"I'm moving in!" Leah clapped her hands together. "Or, should I say, moving back? It still feels like home after all this time. I never thought I'd come back here, but with Mum's death, and—"

"E-Emily's *dead*?"

"Oh." Leah raised her hands to her mouth again. "You haven't heard, then? I suppose you should come in. I'd offer you tea, but I haven't been to the shop yet."

Julia handed over the bag in mute silence before following Leah into the cottage. All of Emily's things were where she had left them. Framed watercolour paintings hung on the walls, and porcelain ornaments covered every surface. If not for the dust, Julia could imagine Emily had merely popped into the village to pick up a loaf of bread.

"Mum passed away two months ago." Leah filled the kettle at the sink. "Cancer. It all happened so quickly."

"Two *months* ago?" Julia echoed, the shock evident in her voice. "I can't believe nobody mentioned it. Surely somebody here knew? She had so many friends in the village."

Leah exhaled as she set the kettle on its base. Plucking two cups from the rack, she swilled them under some warm water while the kettle bubbled.

"Mum was stubborn," Leah said, unable to look Julia in the eyes. "She made us promise not to contact anyone in Peridale. She was humiliated. She hardly left under the best circumstances, did she? She told us all about that nasty business with the Peridale Green Fingers and all those deaths. She never forgave herself for all the lies she told." Leah looked through the bag and pulled out two of the peppermint and liquorice tea packets. She gave them a cautionary sniff, but appeared to like what greeted her because she ripped them open and dropped them into the cups. "She moved to the coast with her cousin, Bonnie, and settled into life quite nicely down there. She had even started a new rose garden. We all went down for Christmas, but we could tell something wasn't right, but she wouldn't go to the doctors. That's what Mum was like though. She was diagnosed in March after collapsing in the post office while drawing her pension. Died in May. We wanted to send something to the paper up here, but she had made us promise not to, and it didn't feel right to betray a dead woman's promise."

Julia's stomach writhed with guilt. Even though she hadn't given Emily cancer, she had been involved in uncovering Emily's plot to fraudulently become the president of the Peridale Green Fingers society. Emily's lies to get to the top had resulted in the original president's accidental death, leading the president's daughter to kill members of the society in revenge. Because of this, Emily had lived her last months away from the village she adored under a grey cloud of regret.

"Was it peaceful?" Julia swallowed the lump in her throat.

"She went in her sleep. She wouldn't have known what was happening. That's what the doctor said, at least. It's something, I suppose."

The kettle pinged, and Leah filled the cups to the brim. She took them over to the tiny dining table and set them down on the faint layer of dust. They both sat and stared into the dark surface of their teas.

"I'm sorry for your loss," Julia offered. "I know what it's like to lose a parent."

"My mum was old." Leah grabbed Julia's hand. "Yours wasn't. But thank you, Julia. I can't believe we're going to be neighbours after all these years."

Julia couldn't believe it either. Being the same age in a small village, they had gone through school side-by-side. Julia couldn't remember what had led to Leah leaving the village, but they had been fond friends, especially in their teens.

"So, you're really moving in here?" Julia took in Emily's floral and pastel décor, which didn't suit Leah's stylish and modern appearance.

"It needs redecorating." Leah blew on the hot surface of her tea. "She left the house to my brother and me. We were trying to sell it when she was alive, but I don't think people could see past the dated wallpaper and carpets. We talked about dropping the price to get rid of it, but neither of us was that desperate for the money, so we decided to hang onto it until we were sure. The tenancy at my flat ended, and after many bottles of wine and a lot of soul searching, I decided to come back. I'm not sure I've made the right decision, but time will tell." Leah paused to sip her tea before smiling and changing the subject. "So, you run a café in the village? I bet people are lining up around the corner for your baking."

"It does okay," Julia said with a modest smile before taking a sip of her tea. "What about you? Are you looking for a job here?"

"I'm a wedding planner," Leah said, her sparkling green eyes darting to the ring on Julia's left hand. "Is that an engagement ring?"

"Oh." Julia felt her cheeks blush. "It is."

"A pearl?" Leah thumbed the milky stone. "Unusual, but gorgeous. Tell me all about him."

"He's called Barker," Julia started, her cheeks blushing hotter. "He lives with me across the road. He used to live down the lane, but a storm destroyed his cottage, and—it's a long story."

"How modern." Leah winked. "What does he do?"

"He's a writer. Well, he *was* a detective inspector, but he retired to focus on writing. His first book came out earlier this year. It was a national bestseller! He wrote it about a body we found under my café!"

"*The Girl in the Basement*?" Leah coughed, and a drop of tea rolled down her chin. "I have that book! I've *read* that book! That was about you? I thought it all felt strangely familiar. I think I saw him on one of those morning chat shows. He's rather handsome, isn't he?

You've bagged yourself a catch there, Julia. Have you set a date?"

"November third. We only secured it last week. I haven't even started planning yet."

Leah coughed again. After she swallowed her mouthful of tea, she reached out and grabbed Julia's hands.

"It's only *three* months away! Oh, Julia! This is *fate*! I'm a wedding planner, and you have a wedding to plan. Coming back here *was* a good idea. Thank the wine!"

"Oh, I didn't really budget to have—"

"Free of charge!" Leah shook both her hands in front of her face. "Are you kidding me? I insist. Like I said, I'm not without money. There's serious cash in weddings. And besides, you're an old friend, and it will give us the chance to really catch up. It will be the perfect opportunity to show the village what I can do to get the bookings coming in. I should pay you, really. Oh, *please* say yes! Just nod, Julia. There's no wedding planner out there who knows your style like I do. I can already see your vision. I bet you all the tea in China that you want a simple village wedding? You don't want glitz and glam, you want refinement and quality."

"Well, yes," Julia said, silently admitting that she had been feeling nervous about how little planning she had done for the big day. She knew she wanted something simple, but even simple weddings required preparation. "Are you sure? It's a lot to ask of someone."

"Call it a wedding gift!" Leah jumped up and pulled Julia into a hug. "It really *is* great to see you again, Julia. I didn't realise how much I'd missed you."

"It's not just me either," Julia said when the hug broke up. "The whole gang is still around. We all boomeranged back to Peridale at some time or another. You're the last to come back, but you're here now."

"The *whole* gang?" Leah's tone deepened as her brows rose. "Like who?"

"Roxy and Johnny," Julia said, thinking the answer should have been obvious. "We were the Fantastic Four, remember? They're not going to believe this."

Julia waited for excitement to flow from Leah, but Leah's smile emerged looking decidedly fake.

"That's great," Leah said, with all the enthusiasm of someone who had just won 20p on the lottery. "We'll all have to catch up soon. I should get on with the unpacking and cleaning first. I can already feel my allergies playing up. We'll talk soon to get started on the wedding planning, okay? How about I swing by your café tomorrow morning?"

Leah practically forced Julia out of the cottage. Julia tried to think why Leah would be less than enthused at the idea of seeing Roxy and Johnny again, but she drew a blank. She shook it off and chalked it up to Leah being overwhelmed with the huge life changes happening to her.

Either way, Julia felt less anxious about the wedding planning she had been putting off, and because the wedding ball was about to start rolling, she finally had something to keep her mind occupied while Jessie hitchhiked around Australia with 'really cool' strangers.

# 2

The next morning, Julia and Barker peered through the beaded curtain separating the kitchen and café. Leah sat at the table nearest the counter, fixated on bridal magazines. A pen hung from the corner of her mouth as she flicked from page to page; sporadically, she reached for it to jot notes in a large leather notebook.

"Isn't she great?" Julia whispered to Barker. "Please tell me you like her."

"She's awesome." Barker fanned himself with a laminated menu. "When is this heatwave going to end? I feel like I'm sat in warm water."

"You'd be complaining if it was cold." Julia took the menu from him and slapped him on the arm with it. "This is important. If she's helping plan our wedding, you need to like her, or it won't work."

A thoughtful expression crossed Barker's face as a glistening bead of sweat escaped his hairline and trickled down his cheek. He attempted to wipe it away, but it rolled into his stubble.

"If you like her, I like her," Barker said, his unsure expression letting Julia know he was trying to say the right thing. "She's an old friend of yours, so you know her better than I do."

"I suppose." Leah reached into her bag to pull out another magazine. "This is her job. She'll know wedding planning better than both of us combined."

"Even Mowgli knows wedding planning better than I do." Barker shook his head as his eyes glazed over. "I have nightmares that you're going to ask me to choose between two shades of beige napkins, and I'm not going to tell the difference, and then you're going to get angry when I pick one at random because it's not the shade of beige you had your heart set on."

Julia slapped him with the menu again. He winked to let her know he was joking, but she heard an element of truth in his quip. From their engagement, Barker had shown little interest in being involved in planning their wedding. He regularly said he would happily marry her at the register office with a handful of close family and friends, and she knew he meant it. It touched her to know that he didn't care about the razzle-dazzle that came with weddings; he only cared about marrying her. Julia wanted just enough razzle-dazzle to give their memories a fuzzy glow when they were old and grey, looking back on their special day.

"Make yourself useful and take this tray of sandwiches out to table seven." Julia pulled away from the beaded curtain. "Katie's not shown up yet."

Barker saluted and scooped up the tray, leaving Julia to continue kneading a fresh batch of scone dough. As her fists worked, beads of sweat formed at her temples. She angled her head back, directing them away from the mixture and onto her dress. The ceiling fan was set to its strongest spin, but it only appeared to be blowing the hot air around.

"Sorry, I'm late!" Katie whined as she rushed in through the back door. "Oh, wow! It's hotter in here than out there. How is that possible, Julia?"

"It's a mystery." Julia paused her kneading to dab at her face with a paper towel. "A mystery that won't be solved until the crisp relief of autumn takes over the village."

"I had to keep wiping off my makeup," Katie said as she dramatically fanned herself with the heavy door. "It wouldn't stick where I put it. I used a long-lasting primer, matte foundation, three different powders, and a setting spray that claims to be waterproof, and I'm *still* sweating through it!"

"I have no idea why." Julia offered Katie a paper towel, which she refused. "Mainly because I understood virtually none of what you just said."

Katie closed the back door and dug through the cupboards until she found a packet of coffee filter papers. She tore one into a rectangle and began dabbing at the shiny surface of her makeup.

"Absorbs oil," Katie explained as the white paper turned translucent with her sweat. "I think I'll need the whole pack."

"You're a wealth of information," Julia said with a dry grin. "I'll file that away for future reference."

"I know lots of things." Katie offered a pleased smile. "Coffee as an exfoliator, olive oil as a moisturiser, baking soda as shampoo." Katie opened the freezer and backed into it. *"Sweet relief!"*

Julia chuckled. With Jessie away, Katie had volunteered to step in to help run the café, an offer Julia had cautiously, but gratefully accepted.

"We're not too busy this morning. I think people are scared they're going to melt if they step outside."

"I can relate," Katie said as she assessed her reflection in the stainless-steel fridge surface. "Oh no! My hair has deflated!"

Julia suppressed her laughter as Katie attempted to fluff up her peroxide curls. Julia couldn't imagine putting so much effort into her appearance on a typical day, let alone during one of the hottest heatwaves the country had ever experienced.

Despite them being the same age, Katie Wellington-South was technically Julia's stepmother. She was married to Julia's father, Brian, and was the mother of Julia's nine-month-old brother, Vinnie—not that her incredibly toned stomach, currently displayed by a revealing crop top, showed any signs of the enormous belly she had possessed for most of the previous year. If not for the temperature, Julia might have told Katie that her outfit was inappropriate. As it was, Julia might have worn something similar if she looked anything like Katie.

"How's Jessie?" Katie resumed her blotting. "Is she enjoying Austria?"

"Austra*lia*."

"Is that in Austria?"

Julia measured Katie's perplexed expression, hoping that it would crack. When it only grew more confused, she realised Katie was not joking.

"Not quite."

"Geography was never my subject at school. None of them were, actually."

"Austria is in Europe," Julia said. "Think *The Sound of Music*. Australia is the one with the kangaroos. And yes, she's having a great time. We video called last night. I needed to see her face."

"Aw, you miss her, don't you?" Katie abandoned the freezer and walked to the sink to wash her hands. "I can't imagine what it would be like if Vinnie went to Australia without me."

"Considering he's a baby, that would be quite impressive," Julia teased as she joined Katie in washing her hands. "But, you're right. I miss her a lot. It feels weird waking up knowing she's not in the room next door."

"They grow up so fast." Katie grabbed her bright pink apron, which had her name bedazzled on the front in sparkling crystals. "Vinnie is already forty-one-weeks-old. I don't know where the time's gone."

"You're counting his age in weeks?"

"It's easier to keep track," Katie said with a shrug, before pushing through the beads into the café.

Julia chuckled as she resumed kneading the dough. She wondered if Katie knew how funny she was, or if her humour was an unintentional by-product of her girlish and childlike personality. Julia had kept Katie at arm's length for the first five years of their relationship because of that personality, but Katie's pregnancy had brought them closer together, and now Julia was glad to call Katie a friend.

When the scone mix was perfect, Julia added chocolate chips and almonds and shaped the dough into circular discs on a greased baking tray. Leaving them to bake, she retrieved her phone from her handbag and called Roxy Carter.

"Bit early, isn't it, Julia?" Roxy grumbled on the other end. "It's the summer holidays. This is when teachers sleep. What's up?"

"You'll *never* guess who's moved back to the village," Julia hummed in a sing-song voice, parting the beads to glance at Leah as she wrote something on her notepad. "You'll *literally* never guess."

"Then what's the point in me trying?"

"Because it's fun!"

During the long pause that followed, Julia imagined Roxy sitting up in bed, squinting at the clock and scratching her fiery red hair as she tried to think of a name.

"Michael Jackson?"

"When did Michael Jackson live in Peridale?"

"He *might* have done."

"Roxy…"

"We don't know everything," Roxy protested through a yawn. "Not even you, Julia."

"Well, he's currently dead."

"That's what they *want* you to think!"

"Roxy…"

"Sorry." Roxy let out another deep yawn. "Violet is big into conspiracy theory documentaries at the moment. I think they're seeping into my brain. Did you know we're all alien lizards from another planet?"

"I didn't," Julia said, unable to conceal her smile at her best friend's dry humour. "Did *you* know coffee filter papers make good sweat absorbers?"

"See, you really *do* learn something new every day," Roxy said, as the distinctive sound of a toilet flushing echoed in the background. "It's fun to share facts."

"Did you just use the bathroom while on the phone to me?"

"What did I *just* say?" Roxy's smirk radiated through the phone. "It's fun to share."

"You're gross."

"Believe it or not, you're not the first to say that."

"I'm shocked." Julia feigned a gasp. "Back to my guessing game."

"So, I wasn't right?"

"It's *still* not Michael Jackson."

"He could be living next door to any of us."

"With Elvis?"

"*Exactly!*" Roxy laughed. "Now you're getting it!"

"Oddly, you're getting warmer." Julia peered into the oven as she sandwiched the phone between her ear and shoulder. "Guess who just moved back into the cottage next door to mine?"

"Emily?"

"Not quite." A lump rose in Julia's throat, but she decided not to mention the former resident's death over the phone, especially since Roxy was still in a sleepy state talking about Michael Jackson's supposed fake death and alien lizard people. "But you're close. Guess again."

Roxy sighed and groaned. Julia imagined her

pacing her bedroom as she pulled on fresh clothes, resigning herself to the reality of her ruined lie-in.

"It's too early for this, Julia! We don't all enjoy playing detective. I haven't even had my morning coffee yet. Tell me, or else I'll hang up and block your number until you can learn to call at a more civilised hour."

Julia wet a cloth and began wiping the counter down, leaving enough of a pause to build up the drama.

*"Leah Burns!"* Julia's voice quivered with excitement. "Remember? Leah from school? She's just moved into her mum's empty cottage."

Another long pause was followed by a click, and then the long hum of a dead phone line.

*"Roxy?"*

Julia waited for Roxy to call back in case she had accidentally ended the call with her cheek. When a minute had ticked by, Julia tapped on Roxy's number again and put the phone to her ear; it diverted straight to voicemail.

"Weird," Julia said aloud, tapping her phone against her chin.

Once the scones were perfectly baked, Julia transferred

them to a cooling rack. Plucking one out, she put it onto a plate with some jam and cream and took it through to the café.

"On the house," Julia said to Leah. "You might want to wait for it to cool down, but I quite like them a little warm."

"You're spoiling me," Leah said after finishing her third cup of free tea. "You're also turning me into a peppermint and liquorice addict. This stuff is delicious." Putting down the cup, Leah thumbed through the magazines crowding the table until she found her notepad. "Okay, so I've started putting together a list of things, in order of importance, we should start brainstorming. I've phoned a few places, like caterers, cake makers, wedding DJs, just to get some prices so we can fit them into your budget."

"You can scratch off cake maker." Julia peered at the upside-down list. "I'll make my own cake."

Leah considered Julia's remark for a moment before crossing it off.

"If you were a normal client, I'd say you were crazy, but I don't think anyone else could bake a wedding cake like you. That frees up a nice chunk of the budget. People charge an arm and a leg for wedding cakes. We can funnel that money into the dress—which reminds me, we should really start looking at dresses as soon as possible. Alterations can take weeks—sometimes months—if things go wrong, and that's provided you find *the* dress at all. Nobody ever believes me when I tell this story, but I had a bride shopping for her dress the day before her wedding because she couldn't decide. She ended up in an ill-fitting poufy ivory number that she swore was *the* dress, but I think she was trying to convince herself that she had done the right thing ignoring my daily warnings."

"I promise I'll listen to all your warnings."

"Good!" Leah laughed before turning to her notes again. "Is that little bridal shop still open on Mulberry Lane?"

"It was the last time I checked."

"Then we'll start there." Leah scribbled down a note. "We don't have to buy from there, but it's a good place to get an idea of what suits your body. I've already marked out some silhouettes and styles I think you'll like, but they're just preliminary ideas."

Leah flicked through a few of the magazines, pausing to show Julia dresses she had circled. They were demure, tasteful, and exactly what Julia had imagined wearing.

"What's all this?" Katie asked, appearing behind

Leah's shoulder. "Wedding dresses?"

"Leah's an old friend," Julia explained. "Leah, this is Katie, she's my—"

"Stepmother," Katie interrupted, holding out a hand to shake Leah's. "Charmed."

"She's married to my father," Julia explained in a hushed voice. "There's a lot to fill you in on." She turned to Katie, who was peering at the displayed dresses with a sceptical eye. "Leah has just moved back to the village. It turns out she's a wedding planner, so she's offered to help plan mine."

"You've set a date?" Katie asked, clearly taken aback. "Since when?"

"Since last week," Barker chimed in without looking up from his laptop. His fingers tapped away without stopping. "November third."

"Oh." Katie's bottom lip quivered. "I see. You know I could have helped you plan your wedding. I planned mine."

Julia felt thoughtless for not anticipating the hurt in Katie's eyes. Katie had been talking about the wedding more than Julia had since Barker's Christmas Day proposal.

"It all happened so quickly," Julia explained, her cheeks prickling. "I didn't want to overload your plate.

You've got Vinnie, and the fake tan business, and you look after your father, and Leah's a professional, and—"

"But *my* wedding was perfect," Katie said, sulking. "Everyone said so."

Julia nodded, although 'perfect' was not the word she would have used to describe it. Six years later and she could still vividly see Katie's pink dress, which, at the time, Julia had said looked like someone had stitched Princess Diana's dress to Cinderella's, doubled the shoulders and ruffles, and then dropped it into a vat of fuchsia dye. Added to an equally pink carriage, horses with pink manes, and her father's white suit and a pink tie, it was not what Julia had in mind for her simple village wedding.

"I'd love your input, Katie," Leah said, nodding at Julia as though she ought to be left alone to pacify the child. "There's room for everyone in a wedding. Oh, I *love* your lipstick! What shade is that?"

"Candy Yum Yum," Katie said, a smile pricking her inflated lips. "Let me take that empty cup."

Katie retrieved the cup and headed into the kitchen. Barker looked up from his laptop and breathed a sigh of relief while Julia stared at Leah in dumbfounded silence.

"It comes with the job," Leah explained. "Working my first wedding, I learned that everyone wants their say. Those with 'step' or 'in-law' before or after their names are usually the worst. It's better to let them *think* they're helping, even if we don't use their ideas. You have the final say on everything, okay? That's how I operate. As long as you're smiling when everyone has left at the end of the wedding, I've done my job correctly."

"I feel like an angel sent you back to Peridale," Julia said, resting a hand on Leah's shoulder. "I can't believe you're doing this for free."

"These cakes are payment enough." Leah picked up her knife and spread the jam onto the scone, followed by the cream. "You really haven't lost your touch."

Julia was about to leave Leah to the rest of her information gathering when the failed phone call to Roxy sprang to mind. If the call had been an isolated incident, Julia might have pushed the thought away, but Leah's reaction to hearing their friends were still in the village ensured there was more to the story than Julia knew.

"I called Roxy," Julia said as casually as she could. "I told her you were back."

Leah stopped chewing the scone for a moment, her eyes freezing on Julia before flicking down to her list. She quickly swallowed the mouthful and licked her lips, her brows tensing.

"Oh?"

"She hung up on me." Julia wondered if she was barking up the wrong tree. "Maybe her phone died? I don't know. Did something happen before you left?"

Without missing a beat, Leah shook her head and said, "Not that I can remember."

Julia nodded, leaving Leah to enjoy the rest of her scone. Julia didn't need powers of detection to know Leah had just lied to her.

She tried Roxy's phone again, but it continued to go to the voicemail message. While Katie used a pocket mirror to reapply her hot pink lipstick, Julia scrolled to another contact, deciding to try another approach.

"*Johnny!*" Julia cried cheerfully. "Are you out and about? Oh, you are? Drop by the café. I have a surprise for you."

Before Johnny could ask any questions, she hung up. Julia smiled at Katie, who beamed back, their earlier wedding-related friction already a distant memory. If Jessie were there, she would have accused Julia of being 'up to something', but, just this once, even though she missed Jessie, Julia was glad her scheming was going unnoticed.

As expected, newspaper journalist Johnny Watson, arrived at the café via the back door fifteen minutes later, his camera strung around his neck. He looked around the empty kitchen and fiddled with his thick-rimmed glasses.

"Hey," he said, his hand drifting up to his brown ringlet curls. "I was just at the village hall taking pictures of the summer trampoline kid's club for the paper. What's going on? You said you had a surprise?"

Julia pushed a slice of carrot cake across the counter and nodded at Johnny to try it. He arched a brow before lifting the cake off the plate. His stiff expression relaxed as soon as his lips closed around the cake.

"S'good," he mumbled before wiping his lips. "Is that citrus?"

"Orange zest. I've been experimenting."

"It's really nice." Johnny placed the unfinished slice back on the counter, his bushy brows pinching together. "You called me here to try your new cake? No offence, Julia, but I come in and buy them at least three times a week. What's the emergency?"

"Ah," Julia said, snapping her fingers together. "You've caught me. I was just trying to butter you up a little, or should I say 'buttercream' you up?"

Julia laughed, but Johnny only smiled awkwardly.

"Anyway." Julia clapped her hands. "There's someone I want you to see."

"Who?"

Julia had been wondering how to reintroduce Johnny to Leah without startling him. From what she could remember, they had all been the best of friends at school, and even though they had drifted apart during their college and university years, Julia struggled to pin down a source for Roxy's frostiness. Johnny, on the other hand, was kind to everyone. She was sure he would be happy to see their old friend.

"Wasn't high school great?" Julia asked with a content sigh. "Those were the days, weren't they?"

"I was overweight, I had acne, and I was too smart for the popular kids, so they bullied me relentlessly," Johnny said, his cheeks reddening. "I'd rather not remember those days, if it's all the same. I've spent the best part of the past two decades blocking it all out."

"But *we* were friends," Julia reminded him. "And Roxy, too. And other people. Does anyone else spring to mind when I say, 'high school friend'?"

"I was friends with Paul. Paul Lucas."

"Do you mean *Mr* Lucas, the chemistry teacher?" Julia snorted. "You can't count teachers as friends, Johnny. No one else?"

"I really do need to get back to the village hall." Johnny hooked his thumb over his shoulder and took a step back. "Thanks for the cake."

Julia grabbed Johnny's hand and dragged him through the beads and into the café. The moment his eyes landed on Leah, the skin around them crinkled, as Julia's had, but instead of breaking into a smile, his mouth twisted into a scowl. His nostrils flared, and his skin turned a deep shade of claret. Julia had never seen Johnny like this in all the years she had known him.

"*Johnny?*" she muttered, trying to snap him out of his trance. "What's wrong?"

"Is this some kind of sick joke?" he snapped, the venom clear in his voice. "I thought better of you, Julia."

"What's wrong?"

"I do not want to talk about this, Julia. Not now. Not ever. Promise me?"

Unnoticed by Leah, still deep in her magazine research, Johnny stormed out of the café before Julia could promise anything. Julia choked on her words as she stared at Barker, gawking curiously in her direction.

"Can you take an hour off tomorrow for the dress shopping?" Leah called out, scribbling something on her notepad without looking up. "Around noon?"

"Sure," Julia said, trying to disguise the wobble in her voice. "Sounds perfect."

# 3

When Katie realised she couldn't tag along for the dress shopping, she offered to open the café and watch things until Julia was finished browsing with Leah. Julia knew Katie was disappointed to be missing out, so she assured her she would be there the next time they looked at dresses.

Julia woke early the next morning and followed Leah's advice to avoid bloating by eschewing a big meal. After a cup of peppermint and liquorice, which she knew would help reduce any expansion from the Chinese takeaway Barker had insisted on ordering the night before, Julia retreated to the garden and video called Jessie.

Their conversation was even briefer than their last, with Jessie hurriedly informing Julia that they were staying on a stud farm with a 'really cool couple', and that she had ridden 'four massive horses' and only been 'chucked off two.' Billy had a terrible sunburn that looked like a 'really burnt lasagne', and Alfie was 'badly chatting up every girl he made eye contact with.' With an assurance that she was having 'tons of fun' and being 'as safe as houses', Jessie said she would 'call soon-ish.' Instead of Jessie's face and voice soothing her, each call only cultivated Julia's creeping anxiety about her daughter's absence.

With Barker in the dining room, working on his second novel, Julia showered and dressed for the day ahead. When she set off to Leah's cottage at half past eleven, she was pleased to see Leah already locking up. Leah wore a vibrant yellow blouse and high-waisted, figure-hugging jeans. It was a look Julia couldn't pull off, but Leah was doing it with ease.

"Your car or mine?" Julia asked, swinging her keys around her forefinger. "Or we can walk?"

"Are you kidding me?" Leah slapped Julia on the shoulder and directed her towards Julia's vintage, aqua-blue Ford Anglia. "I've been dying to take a spin in this retro beauty since I arrived."

Wanting to give Leah the full experience, Julia took the scenic route into the village, heading up the lane and circling around Peridale Farm. During the drive, they talked about everything that had happened in the last twenty years. Leah had married young, divorced young, remarried, and divorced again. She had entered her thirties realising she only enjoyed planning weddings, not living with the result of them. She was childless, but claimed not to regret it, and had spent the last decade in York, the most eligible yet unattainable bachelorette in town, focussed on providing fairy tales and not living them. When Leah ran out of breath, Julia shared all about her time living in London, her failed twelve-year marriage, her return to Peridale, opening her café, her initially frosty relationship with Barker, and her chance meeting with Jessie.

"Adoption?" Leah asked, smiling softly. "You always were the kindest person I knew. Not many people would take in a kid off the streets and do that, you know?"

"I'd like to think more people would than you'd imagine."

"You always see the best in people." A hint of sadness tinged Leah's voice. "I wish I were more like that. After all the drama I've been through, you grow suspicious of everyone. I think that's why we've clicked again like no time has passed. We've known each other since before the messiness of adulthood. Our friendship is unspoiled."

As they pulled into Mulberry Lane, Julia wondered if she was choosing to see the best in Leah. She had spent most of the night trying to contact Roxy and Johnny to get to the bottom of their reactions, but evidently, they had taken a vow of silence. After attempting to call them each a dozen times, she dove twenty years into her memory to recall the cause of the strain, but she drew a blank no matter what angle she came at the problem from.

She remembered Leah being there when she left high school and started her patisserie and baking course at college, but they had drifted apart, and life had swept them in different directions. Whatever issues Johnny and Roxy had with Leah, Julia was sure she hadn't been involved in them.

Whatever had happened all those years ago, Julia

was sure they could smooth things out with a little time. She selfishly wanted her old gang back together, even if they were all on the tipping edge of forty. So much had changed in her life since those days, and yet it was comforting to know something old could become new again. Like Emily's unruly rose garden, their friendship just needed a little pruning. Julia had already decided to bluntly ask Leah for the truth after they were finished with the day's wedding task. For the time being, Julia was going to try and enjoy dressing up as much as someone who only wore one of ten revolving vintage dresses could.

Climbing out of the car, Julia gazed up at the bridal shop as the afternoon sun beat down on them. She could already feel sweat mocking the shower she had taken only an hour ago.

*"Brooke's Bridal Boutique?"* Leah read aloud, an air of unease surrounding her. "Brooke is a common name, isn't it?"

"Does it matter?" Julia asked.

Leah parted her lips to say something, but she was cut off by a voice calling them from up the street. They turned to see Julia's sister, Sue, and her gran, Dot, walking arm-in-arm towards them. Dot waved at Julia with a beaming grin, her eyes narrowing warily when they landed on Leah.

"Something tells me this isn't a coincidence," Julia said, sighing as she shielded her eyes from the sun.

"There are no coincidences in life, dear." Dot kissed Julia on the cheek. "I ran to the café to tell you some dreadful news and Katie told me where you were. You kept that quiet, didn't you? Wedding dress shopping without *us*? I called Sue immediately! Jessie has been gone for a week, and your brain has already turned to mush. And you're not looking the best." Dot rested her hand on Julia's forehead. "You're clammy. Are you feeling okay?"

"We're in the middle of a heatwave, Gran." Julia batted the hand away. "And before you say it, no, I'm still *not* perimenopausal."

"Neil has the twins all day." Sue let out a thrilled squeal. "Which means we can spend the whole afternoon looking at dresses! Isn't that exciting, Julia?"

"As long as they have air-conditioning." Julia wiped the gathering droplets from her forehead. "I'm melting."

"I don't sweat," Dot announced as she adjusted her brooch. "Never have. I don't think I know how. The doctors called me a medical mystery. They'll probably want my body for science when I finally pop my clogs."

Sue and Julia looked at each other, and it took all their strength not to laugh.

"You say some strange things, Gran," Julia said, shaking her head. "What was this urgent, tragic news you were dying to tell me?"

"Dying is the *right* word!" Dot opened her arms with a flourish. "Amy heard from Shilpa who heard from Father David who heard from Evelyn that Emily Burns is *dead*! Cancer, apparently. She escaped death during that whole Green Fingers mess, and now she's up there with the other members that died thanks to her lying. How I'd *love* to be a fly on the wall of *that* reunion. I'd say she got what she—"

Julia cleared her throat, cutting her gran off with a weighty shake of her head. She couldn't bring herself to look at Leah.

"I didn't have a chance to introduce my wedding planner," Julia said. "Or should I say, reintroduce. You remember Leah, don't you, Gran? Leah *Burns*. Emily's *daughter*."

Dot's eyes widened, and she took a cautionary step back. Her wobbly fingers fiddled with her brooch as her lips attempted to form words.

"Of c-c-course," Dot said with a strained smile, her voice taking on a sweet tone that sounded altogether foreign. "Forgive me, dear. One can lose one's marbles upon achieving a certain age, if you know what I mean."

"Calm down, Queen Elizabeth," Sue said through almost gritted teeth before gesturing to the shop in front of them. "*Dresses!* They won't try themselves on, will they? Now, if one wants to remove one's foot from one's mouth?"

Sue dragged Dot towards the front door, but not before a feeble 'sorry for your loss' escaped her gran's lips. When the bell rang, and the door closed behind them, embarrassment seized Julia, and she wanted nothing more than for the pavement to swallow her up.

"Don't apologise." Leah held up both hands before Julia could speak. "I was expecting as much eventually. It's nothing my mother didn't say about herself. Shall we go in?"

"Yes." Julia inhaled deeply. "And if she says anything else, I promise I'll banish her from any future wedding-related activities."

"Deal. I must admit, I was a little shocked to see your gran still alive. I'm sure Dot was in her eighties when we were kids. Her hundred-and-fourth birthday must be coming up any day now."

Leah's wink told Julia there were no hard feelings. Holding the door open, Leah let Julia enter the boutique first. Julia was delighted when an icy blast of air conditioning hit her in the face. She was less than surprised to find Dot and Sue already sipping champagne with their feet up.

"Grab a glass!" Dot called to Julia as she lifted her flute in the air. "It's *free!*"

"Free to *customers*," Brooke, the owner, said with a tight smile. "Who is the bride-to-be?"

Julia raised a finger, and Brooke crossed the shop to hand her a champagne flute. Julia knew the bridal shop owner's face from around the village, but she couldn't remember ever speaking with her. Brooke had never visited Julia's café, which made her think she lived out of the village and commuted in.

Brooke was a tall, stick-insect of a woman, with a turned-up nose and beady eyes. Her jet-black hair, edges already showing signs of greying, had been pulled back into an uncomplicated bun. Julia suspected they were around the same age, but the severity of Brooke's appearance had prematurely aged her by at least a decade. Brooke's sharp, black suit jacket and pencil skirt didn't help soften her edges; she looked like she was about to sell them coffins, not wedding dresses.

"Do you have a date for the ceremony?" Brooke asked, glancing over Julia's shoulder at Leah, who had already set to work sifting through the racks of dresses. "Please, all in good time. I'm the only one allowed to touch the dresses. For sanitary reasons, of course."

Leah backed away from the dresses and nodded, her back still turned. She squinted up at the ceiling as she rocked on her heels. Dot waved at Julia and made a circular 'cuckoo' motion around her head.

"A date?" Brooke prompted with a tight smile.

"Oh, yes," Julia said after a deep glug of her bubbly champagne. "November third."

"Of *next* year?" Brooke's lips thinned even more.

"*This* year!" Dot cried. "Where's Evelyn with her psychic powers when you need them? She's getting married *this* year. I'll take a top-up, thank you."

Brooke glanced at Dot, but she didn't move to fill up her glass.

"Only the bride and her bridesmaids get a second glass." Brooke's tone was so cutting Julia was surprised the glass in her hand hadn't shattered. "And I assume *you*," she shot Dot a glance, "are *not* a bridesmaid."

Dot pursed her lips and tossed back the rest of her champagne with a sulk. Usually, Julia would have been amused by her gran's antics, but the awkward tension radiating from Leah, who still hadn't turned to face them, was making her wish they hadn't bothered stepping foot into the shop.

"Bridesmaids?" Brooke asked Julia. "These two ladies?"

"Just my sister," Julia said, pointing at Sue. "This is my wedding planner, Leah."

"*Bridesmaid*?" Sue sprung up from her seat. "Did you just say I was a *bridesmaid*?"

While Sue jumped up and down on the spot and clapped like a hyperactive seal, Brooke stalked towards Leah. As if sensing the approaching presence, Leah ducked away and turned to face Julia. The fear in Leah's eyes made Julia's gut wrench.

"Why do I feel like we've just walked into a lion's den?" Julia asked, almost to herself. "*Leah*?"

"Leah," Brooke repeated, her lips snarling, much like Johnny's had. "It *is* you. Leah Burns."

Finally, Leah turned to face Brooke. Julia could have heard a pin drop, but instead, she heard the shuffle of ice as Dot pulled the champagne bottle from its metal jug. Her gran crept back to her chair and topped up her glass before resuming her front row seat at the staring contest.

"What's going on?" a male voice called through an open door at the back of the shop. "Mum?"

The words pierced the air with the sharpness of a

gun crack heralding the beginning of a dog race. Julia was sure her eyes had accessed a new slow-motion mode because she saw the exact moment Brooke cracked. With a guttural, primitive scream, the shop owner launched at Leah, grabbing fistfuls of her hair. Leah copied this, grabbing Brooke's black up-do, loosening up the bun to reveal hair long enough to rival Rapunzel's.

Julia attempted to wedge herself between the women, but they had reached a stalemate, neither letting go.

"*Mum!*" the young man cried again, his deep voice booming around the tiny shop. "Stop this!"

Like his mother, the new arrival was tall, almost skeletal, with limbs that seemed impossibly stretched out. He had shaggy ebony hair, which would have scraped the ceiling if he stood on tiptoes. His youth smoothed the edges he'd obviously inherited from his mother.

"*Leah!*" Julia muttered through gritted teeth as she tried to pry Leah's hands away from Brooke's hair. "Leah, let go!"

But Leah simply grunted and gripped even tighter, forcing Julia to resort to a self-defence trick Barker had taught her. She grabbed the underside of Leah's arms and pinched with her nails deep into the muscle. Not enough to break the skin, but enough to hurt. Leah cried out and let go, and the shock made Brooke release her grip long enough for her son to drag her away.

Immediately, Brooke looked ready for a second attack. It took her son pinning her against a rack of dresses and gripping her face to break her out of her rabid state.

"Stop," he said sternly. "What's got into you?"

"That's *Leah*!" she cried, pointing across the shop as a slither of spit flew from her knotted mouth. "Leah Burns, Max! That's *her*."

Max turned to face the dishevelled wedding planner. His face twisted into the perfect reflection of his mother's, causing Julia's heart to drum faster than it ever had; she was not too proud to admit she was scared. She stood in front of Leah and spread out her arms, much to Dot's horrified dismay, if the gasps meant anything. Julia waited for mother and son to launch a fresh attack, but it didn't come.

Max stood in front of his mother, mirroring Julia's stance. He stared through Julia to the cowering new arrival. He pointed to the door, lips twisted in a grimace.

"Leave."

They didn't need to be told twice. Sue and Dot darted for the door, Dot still clutching the champagne bottle to her chest. Julia pushed Leah into the street, the bright afternoon sun blinding her. She was relieved when she heard the lock click behind them and the sign slap from 'OPEN' to 'CLOSED'.

"I haven't felt that alive since the war!" Dot cried, her hand on her chest as she panted for breath. "Crikey!"

"Which war?" Sue asked, also panting.

"I don't know." Dot paused to swig from the champagne bottle. "All of them! What *was* that?"

Julia looked at Leah for an explanation, but it was clear she had entered shutdown mode. Julia gripped her friend's shoulders and tried to force their eyes to meet, but Leah was somewhere else entirely.

"I thought people would have moved on," Leah mumbled, her voice buried deep in her throat. "It's been twenty years."

"Moved on from *what*?" Julia shook Leah's shoulders out of sheer frustration. "What happened?"

Leah's eyes snapped onto Julia's long enough for her to know she was not going to find out the truth. Leah pulled away and set off up the street, but she stopped in her tracks when she came face to face with

Roxy and Violet, who were walking hand-in-hand down Mulberry Lane. They were in their own summer afternoon bubble, so blissfully unaware of the chaos around them that they didn't notice Leah until they were about to bump into her. Leah and Roxy stepped back at the same time, leaving Violet where she had stopped. Without saying a word, Roxy doubled back and sprinted up the lane, leaving Violet behind.

"*Leah*!" Julia called after her. "Please tell me what all this is about!"

"You're Leah?" Violet cried, her Russian accent turning the air cold as a familiar snarl took over her lips. She looked Leah up and down before shaking her head. "You do not belong here. Go back to where you came from, vile woman."

Violet spat at Leah's feet before running after Roxy, who had already disappeared around the corner.

"Why do I feel like everyone knows what's going on *except* for me?" Julia cried, a little louder than she had intended. "Leah?"

But Leah only dropped her head, crossed the street, and turned the corner. Julia considered chasing after her, but as though she could sense it, Dot pulled her back.

"Let her go." Dot hiccoughed and looked down at

the almost empty bottle in her hand. "I'd be surprised if this is even real champagne. I can taste quality, and this is definitely the £2.50 fizzy wine from the corner shop."

"You seemed to enjoy it," Sue muttered. "I can't believe this is how I'm spending my first child-free afternoon in months."

"The night is still young!"

Julia checked her watch. "It's only half past noon."

"Exactly!" Dot slapped the hood of Julia's car before climbing inside. "To the pub, driver!" She rolled down the window and peered up at Sue. "Unless you have something better to do?"

Sue shrugged and joined Dot in the backseat.

Julia frowned. The first milestone of her wedding planning had been ruined, she was no closer to having a dress, and she was leaving Mulberry Lane with more questions about Leah than she had arrived with.

# 4

J ulia spent the rest of the day at the café, hopelessly distracted. She served Shilpa Patil a teapot minus the tea bags, Evelyn Wood a sandwich consisting solely of lettuce, and Amy Clark soft cheese instead of cream for her chocolate chip scone. When the time came to close the café, Julia had never been so glad to flip the sign and lock the doors.

Unfortunately for Barker, her level of concentration didn't improve when she returned to the cottage. The shepherd's pie she attempted to make was given an unsavoury twist when she accidentally used curry powder instead of gravy granules. Despite Barker's protests of enjoyment, she knew he had forced down every mouthful.

"Let's go for a walk," Barker suggested after clearing the failed dinner from the dining room table. "The fresh air will do you a world of good."

Julia hoped Barker would be right, but her mind was firmly fixed on one subject: Leah Burns. She bit her tongue and listened to Barker's book updates for the first ten minutes of their sunset stroll, but when the path disappeared into the fields surrounding Peridale Farm, she couldn't help but turn the conversation to the bridal shop confusion.

"It was like watching animals fight," Julia said. "The Leah I knew wasn't like that."

"The Leah you knew left Peridale a long time ago." Barker looped his arm through Julia's and offered a supportive smile. "Let's hope you're not going to be dragged in as an assault witness anytime soon."

"I don't know *what* I witnessed."

"A fight?"

"It was *more* than that." Julia gazed at a flock of wandering sheep in a neighbouring field. "And why?

Why did Brooke launch herself at Leah? Why did Roxy run away? Why did Violet spit at her feet? Why did Johnny act like an entirely different person when he saw her? What did she do that was so terrible? Who is she?"

"Who *was* she?"

"She was lovely." Julia let out a long sigh as the warm breeze fluttered her hair from behind her ears. "She was polite and kind. As far as I knew, everyone loved her. People used to call her the 'teacher's pet' because she was always the first to volunteer for anything. She once missed a party to help Mrs Dawson clean her textbook cupboard after school, but that's the type of person she was. She didn't care if people thought that made her a geek, she just liked to help. If you needed anything, whether it be homework help or a shoulder to cry on, Leah was the one to jump in. She was a good friend. Her offer to plan our wedding for free was typical Leah. That's precisely what she would do. She wasn't a wicked troublemaker."

"That's one version of her," Barker suggested. "But as you know, people have different sides to them. If my years in the police force taught me anything, it's that you can't take anyone at face value. I've seen sweet and demure people snap over trivial things. We all have it in us to hurt others." They slowed to a halt and leaned against a fence to watch a nearby grazing horse. "My guess is, she came back to Peridale hoping time had healed old wounds, but for Roxy and Johnny and the dress shop lady, it sounds like they needed another twenty." Barker paused and broke his gaze from the horse to look at Julia. "And do you know what that tells us?"

"What?"

"Whatever she did must have been quite terrible."

Julia took in a deep lungful of the warm evening air. Barker had hit the nail on the head.

"But what if Leah has changed?" Julia's teeth worried at her bottom lip as the horse shook out its mane and neighed. "So, she did something awful twenty years ago. She would have been eighteen when she left the village. She's thirty-eight now, like me. I know I'm not the same person I was at eighteen. Are you?"

Barker shook his head.

"People *can* change." Julia tapped her finger on the fence with each word. "Isn't forgiveness important?"

"It is." Barker pulled his arm away from Julia's and looped his fingers together, leaning over the fence. She knew the expression on his face. He was about to tell her something she absolutely didn't want to hear. "But it's not your place to demand that forgiveness. Twenty years may have passed, but it doesn't mean she shouldn't be held accountable for whatever she did."

She tried to think of an appropriate reply as the horse sauntered toward them, its chestnut coat glowing under the setting sun. The longer Barker's words hung in the air, the more she knew there was no point in attempting to counter them. If Leah had been the kind and helpful friend in their group, Julia had always been 'The Fixer'. It was in her nature to make everyone around her happy, and that need could quickly blind her.

"You're right." Julia reached out to stroke the horse's long nose. "Maybe this isn't my fight. I wanted so desperately to get the old gang together, but what will it cost if I push it? If Roxy and Johnny can't even look at Leah without foaming at the mouth, it's going to take more than my meddling to fix it."

"You? *Meddle*?" Barker winked and nudged Julia's shoulder. "Never."

She laughed as she coiled her arm back through his. They left their equine friend to finish his sunset grazing and circled around Peridale Farm before joining the winding lane that led back to their cottage. When the lights of Julia's sitting room came into view, the sky above them was an almost perfect blanket of darkness speckled with stars.

"What if Roxy and Johnny never speak to me again?" Julia broke the silence, her voice barely above a whisper. "I've agreed to let Leah plan our wedding, but, obviously, I want Roxy and Johnny to be part of it. I was going to ask Roxy to be one of my bridesmaids. I've barely thought about Leah in the past two decades, and even though it's been nice to see her, Roxy and Johnny have always been there in some capacity."

"Exactly." Barker nodded. "They're not going to abandon you. You had noble intentions, as you always do. And don't forget, you still don't know what happened."

"Things would make *much* more sense if I did."

"So, find out."

"How?"

They stopped at their garden gate. Barker nodded in the direction of Leah's cottage, where soft light poured out into the dark garden.

"It looks like she's home." Barker pulled Julia away from their cottage and back onto the lane. "It's time you asked her for the truth."

"What if she doesn't want to give it?"

"Then you've got your answer. If Leah isn't mature enough to be honest with you about something that happened years ago, your friendship isn't going to work. But, something tells me she wouldn't have come back here if she didn't want to live peacefully."

As they approached Leah's cottage, Julia immediately knew something was not right. The front door was slightly open, and the light flooding into the garden was coming from the floor, not the ceiling. Barker glanced cautiously at Julia.

"Wait here." He put his arm in front of her and unhooked the gate. "It's probably nothing."

"If it's nothing, I don't need to wait anywhere." She slipped through the gate before he had a chance to push it back into its latch. "Although something tells me this isn't nothing."

They crept up the garden path like two teenagers venturing towards a haunted house on Halloween. Julia's gaze was fixed on the yellow light seeping through the bottom of the open door. Its stillness and concentrated lines unsettled her in ways she couldn't explain.

"*Leah?*" Barker called out, the boom in his voice making Julia jump.

They lingered on the step, their ears directed at the

door. The seconds thudded like rocks dropping into a shallow pond.

"Maybe she's not here?" Barker glanced back at the lane where Leah's car was. "She might have gone for a walk."

"*Leah?*" Julia called, hoping the familiarity of her voice would stir movement in the cottage. "Are you in? It's Julia. I only want to talk."

They waited again, but no sound came. Unable to take the silence a moment longer, Julia reached out with her forefinger and pushed on the door. It swung back on its hinges, revealing the source of the strange light. A table lamp lay on the floral carpet, its dusty shade bent out of shape. The sight of something so ordinary should have eased Julia, but the matching smashed vase and decapitated Little Bo-Peep figurine pointed to something more sinister.

"These were all on this side table." Julia pointed to the long, walnut cabinet under a mirror on the hallway wall. "I'm sure of it." She paused, the realisation of the scene hitting her. "It looks like someone's had a fight."

"The explanation could be harmless," Barker said, his tone giving away the suspicion in his voice. "But yes, it looks like the result of a scuffle." He stepped over the broken items and peered up the staircase into the darkness of the landing. *"Leah?"*

If Leah had been asleep, Barker's echoing call would have woken her. Julia waited for a sign of movement above, but the floorboards didn't so much as creak. Stepping over the lamp, she walked into the kitchen. Flickering blue light illuminated the room from a lit gas ring under a hissing pan. After clicking on the ceiling light, Julia investigated further. The pan was empty, and the metal bottom sizzled, hinting at a drop of remaining moisture. Julia grabbed the handle, a scream escaping her throat when she dropped the scorching metal onto the kitchen tiles.

"I should have known." Julia held out the pink burn on her palm when Barker dashed into the kitchen. "It looks like she was boiling water to cook something. It'd completely evaporated."

Julia scanned the kitchen. Barker gestured toward the opened bottle of white wine just as Julia's gaze landed on it. Two empty glasses stood next to it.

Clutching her wrist, Julia ran her palm under the cold water. A mobile phone and a bunch of keys sat next to the sink.

"This isn't right," Julia called to Barker, who was back in the hallway, staring at the scattered objects on the floor. "I think we need to call the police."

"I think you're right." Barker beckoned for Julia to join him. "I don't think this is part of the carpet design."

Wiping her wet hand on a paper towel, Julia walked into the hallway. She stared where Barker was pointing, but her eyes couldn't see anything other than flowers in the glow of the broken lamp. She shook her head, prompting him to circle a dark patch. Julia thought it was a rose in the cluttered design until she realised it was wet and glistening in the light.

"Blood," she choked. "Barker, that's blood."

Barker's expression darkened as he pulled his phone from his pocket. He tapped on the screen and put the device to his ear, his eyes fixed on Julia.

"John? It's Barker. Yeah, I'm fine—sort of. I need you to come look at something. Yeah, now. Yes, it's important. Yes, it's more important than your pint."

Leaving Barker to explain what they had found to his former colleague, Julia returned to the kitchen, her hand on her forehead as she tried to wrap her mind around what they had just stumbled upon. Something red on the glossy bannister caught her attention. She parted her lips to tell Barker she had found more blood, but she stopped when she realised what she was staring at might have been the colour of blood, but it was something else entirely. It was a hair, and there was only one person in the village with hair that fiery. Julia's gut twisted as her mind jumped to conclusions faster than she was comfortable with.

"He's coming up with a team," Barker said after tucking his phone back into his pocket. "Julia?"

Julia swiped the hair into her fist as she spun around, her heart drumming. She stuffed her hand into her pocket and tried to banish the shock from her face.

"Don't worry," Barker said softly as he pulled her into his chest. "I know what you're thinking, but there's no point getting worked up yet. This could all be nothing."

"I know."

But Julia's mind was thinking something else entirely. With the red hair clenched in her burnt palm, only one thought circled relentlessly through her mind:

*Roxy has killed Leah.*
*Roxy has killed Leah.*
*Roxy has killed Leah.*

# 5

"**R**oxy Carter, you should know better than to ignore my calls." Julia paced the tiny stone yard behind her café. "I know you're listening to these messages. You're too curious not to. I know where you were last night. Call me back *immediately* before you get yourself into a situation you can't get out of. I only want to talk."

Julia hung up and reached into her apron pocket. She pulled out the plastic zip-lock bag containing the red hair. What had possessed her to take the hair from Leah's house? She grabbed her phone again.

"Roxy, it's still me," Julia muttered into her phone after calling for the thirteenth time that morning. "You have no idea how much I'm putting my neck on the line for you right now. Call me back, or, better yet, *answer* your phone!"

Julia hung up again, her anger increasing with each new message. It was not like Roxy to ignore her, and yet it was typical of Roxy to bury her head in the sand when things were too serious to deal with. Julia had played over every possible situation that could have occurred at Leah's cottage, and very few scenarios left Roxy in a good place.

"Why were you at Leah's cottage?" Julia spoke to the hair, desperately wanting a reply. "What did you do?"

Tucking the hair back into her pocket, she pulled on the heavy back door and returned to the kitchen, cringing as the sweltering heat hit her. The sun still had its blistering fingers wrapped around the village, and it showed no sign of letting go. The weather was unbearable to work in, but it would have been even more agonising if every customer had been asking Julia about what she had discovered at Emily Burns' old cottage. News of Leah's vanishing act had yet to spread like most Peridale gossip usually did.

After checking her phone—still no messages—Julia pushed through the beaded curtain. A small line had formed at the counter, but it was nothing Katie couldn't handle. Julia had yet to mention what had happened, but Katie was stepping up and taking on Julia's responsibilities regardless.

"I heard police were sniffing around up near the farm," Shilpa Patil whispered to Malcolm Johnson in the queue. "Amy said she saw a white tent in front of Emily's old cottage."

"Emily Burns?" Malcolm replied. "You don't suppose it has anything to do with her death?"

"She died of cancer," Father David jumped in. "Or, that's what I heard, at least. Poor soul."

When Dot burst through the door in her usual hurricane fashion, Julia was glad of the distraction, if only to stop the villagers turning to her for an explanation behind the forensic tent surrounding her closest neighbour's home.

"*Crikey*, Julia!" Dot exclaimed, her hand gripping the brooch holding her collar together as a look of horror spread across her face. "You look like death! The bags under your eyes are like sacks of sugar! Did you sleep?"

"As it happens, I didn't." Julia sighed as she rubbed her tired eyes. "But thank you. I know I can always count on you for a confidence boost."

"Dear?" Dot's expression softened as she pulled Julia away from the counter and into a quiet corner. "Has something happened? Are you and Barker okay?"

"Why wouldn't we be?"

"Wedding planning!" Dot cried. "The stress it causes makes me wonder if the result is worth it. Your grandfather and I could barely look at each other in the week leading up to our nuptials. Well, he did have that lazy eye if the wind was blowing in the wrong direction, but that's another story for another day." Dot paused for breath before her hand lifted to cover her mouth. "It's not Jessie, is it?"

"Jessie's fine," Julia replied. "Well, I assume she is. I haven't spoken to her in a couple of days. I'm trying not to be a worrying mother while she's having the time of her life. No. Something happened with Leah."

"That's funny, I was going to say the *same* thing." Dot squinted as she sat down at the table next to the window. "So, *you* know?"

"Know what?"

"What *I* know."

Julia sat across from her gran, one brow arched as she tried to figure out what she was hinting at. There was not enough coffee in Peridale to make Julia's brain function at full capacity after her sleepless night.

"Gran," Julia said sternly, "what did you rush in here to tell me?"

Dot bit her lip, looking as though the excitement of her news wanted to burst out. Julia assumed they were on different pages of a book, unless Dot was happy Leah had vanished.

"After that commotion at the bridal shop, I went to the pub with Sue, didn't I? After a couple glasses of sherry—"

"A couple?"

"Well, six." Dot pushed a hand through her curls with a satisfied smile. "I might be old, but I'm not dead yet, dear. After all that sherry, my memories loosened up. I knew there was something fishy about that Leah girl, I'd just forgotten what. Do you remember why Leah left Peridale?"

Julia shook her head.

"Not many people seem to," Dot continued. "I took a poll of the people in the pub, and only Amy Clark remembered, but that's because she was attached to Emily's hip. Emily tried to sweep it under the rug, and she did a good job. I think most people even forgot she had a daughter. She was a sneaky woman, God rest her soul." Dot glanced up at the ceiling with puckered lips. "Of course, I heard all about it at the time. You know me, dear. I always have one ear to the ground. Not much gets past me."

"Heard about what?"

Dot smirked as she leaned in, glancing around to make certain no ears were to the ground anywhere near them.

"Leah ran off with an older man," Dot whispered.

"Oh."

"There's more."

"Oh?"

"Leah ran off with an older man," Dot repeated, her smile growing with each word, "on the day of *his* wedding."

"*Oh!*"

"*Exactly!*" Dot cried, startling Shilpa as she walked to the door. "Leah was eighteen and he was in his mid-twenties, if I remember correctly. The rumour was they'd been having an affair for months, and he left his wife at the altar to go gallivanting with a teenaged girl. It would have been quite a scandal, but Emily lied through her teeth and told everyone Leah had gone off to university. There wasn't enough evidence to prove the rumour, so it fizzled out, and people forgot. You know what folk around here are like. They can be a little…" Dot leaned in even further "…*simple.*"

"Leah said she married young and divorced young," Julia thought aloud, her fingers drumming on the table. "So, that would line up. Why have I not heard any of this before?"

"You were busy with college and working all the hours God sent in that bakery. Roxy and Johnny went to university around that time, so maybe you thought she drifted off with them? It doesn't matter. What matters is that I remembered. Mystery solved!"

"Who was the man?"

"Hmmm," Dot said, her face scrunching up. "I don't know. I don't know who the ditched bride was, either. Why don't I know?"

"Maybe they weren't from Peridale?"

"That makes sense." Dot nodded, still deep in thought. "It'll come to me."

Julia waited for Dot's revelation. She looked around the café and watched as Katie cut a giant slice of carrot cake for Father David. It was double what Julia would have sliced, but she decided against interjecting.

"The bridal shop lady!" Dot snapped her fingers

together. "What was her name?"

"Brooke."

"It *has* to be Brooke! She wanted to kill Leah—and she might have done if you hadn't ruined the fun and broke them up. If the woman who ran off with your husband-to-be on the day of your wedding turned up, you'd want to kill her."

"Would I?"

"Well, *I* would," said Dot defiantly. "It makes sense."

Julia could certainly see some sense in Dot's argument. Brooke's reaction lined up with such a situation, but it didn't explain where Roxy and Johnny came into the story.

"So, what do you know?" Dot asked, edging forward. "*Spill!*"

Julia paused, reaching for words that wouldn't come. If she told Dot anything, the information would surely be talked about all over Peridale by teatime.

With perfect timing, Sue burst into the café as Father David left. She had a bottle of champagne in each hand, a pink feather boa around her neck, and two stacks of bridal magazines under each arm.

"*Champagne!*" Katie exclaimed, clapping her hands together. "What's the occasion?"

"Wedding planning!" Sue placed the bottles on one of the empty café's tables before dropping the stacks of magazines. "Just because yesterday was ruined, it doesn't mean we should lose momentum. As an *official* bridesmaid, it's my duty to keep the train moving. Katie, grab some glasses."

Katie teetered into the kitchen with a squeal. Sue skipped over to Julia and wrapped the boa around her neck, loose pink feathers flying into the air around her. One landed in Dot's mouth as she yawned. Dot choked and coughed it out before giving Sue a frosty look. On any other day, Julia would have been touched by Sue's surprise, but today was different. She unravelled the boa and placed it on the table.

"Loosen up, big sis." Sue picked up one of the bottles and popped the cork into the corner of the room. "*Glasses*, Katie!"

Katie hurried back with four latte glasses. Sue directed the foam into them and topped them up, emptying the bottle in one go.

"Where's that wedding planner of yours?" Sue looked around the café with a wrinkled nose. "Licking her wounds, no doubt?"

Julia sighed and collapsed into the nearest chair. She rubbed her temples; a headache was forming rapidly.

"Something happened last night," Julia began, her eyes fixed on the stack of magazines. "I went to Leah's cottage to try and get an explanation out of her, and she wasn't there."

"She's left Peridale *already*?" Dot sounded disappointed. "Spoilsport!"

"Good riddance." Sue lifted her glass before slurping the foam off the top. "You don't need a wedding planner when you have us, does she, girls?"

"Nope," Katie and Dot said in unison.

Julia sighed again. Lightning cracked through her head, threatening to split her skull in two.

"It wasn't just that she wasn't there," Julia continued as she rubbed her swollen eyelids. "It looked like there'd been a struggle of some kind, and there was blood on the carpet."

Sue spat her champagne back into the glass and sat down, her cheeks darkening in an instant.

"She's *d-dead*?"

"I don't know." Julia ran her fingers through her hair and massaged her scalp to try and ease the building tension. "The police are looking for her right now."

"She'll turn up," Dot said airily. "What's the drama? I'd bet my pension that Brooke went back for another brawl. That's all it'll be."

"She left her phone, car and house keys, the front door was open, and she was in the middle of cooking."

"Oh." Dot's face wrinkled. "That's unusual."

"It sounds like she was taken," Katie announced. "I saw something like that in a film."

"What film?" Sue asked.

"*Taken*," Katie replied bluntly.

Sue and Dot rolled their eyes, but it was one of the scenarios Julia had considered during her long, sleepless night. It was one of the gentler scenes because it was one of the few where Leah was still alive.

"There's more," Julia said, reaching into her apron. "I found this in Leah's house."

The trio of women squinted at the red hair in the bag. They exchanged unsure glances, none of them piecing Julia's theory together.

"It's a hair," Sue said.

"Or string?" Katie added.

"No, it's definitely hair," Dot said. "I can tell."

"It's a *red* hair." Julia held the bag up to the window. "How many people do you know with hair like this in Peridale?"

"Well, there's…" Dot's eyes widened as the puzzle pieces joined together. "*Oh*! Roxy?"

"Bingo."

Julia's eyes snapped into focus, looking past the plastic bag and through the window. She saw a tall figure and realised she was parading stolen evidence around in broad daylight. When she realised the figure was Barker, she stuffed the bag back into her apron.

"Hello, ladies," Barker said as he walked into the café, the bell announcing his arrival. "I'm not interrupting anything, am I?"

"I just came to do some wedding planning," Sue said before slurping her champagne.

"And then Julia told us about Leah," Dot added.

"And about that hair of Roxy's she found at Leah's house," Katie said carelessly as she reached for her glass of bubbles. "I wonder if Roxy was the one who took her? I think it was Russians in the movie. Roxy's girlfriend is Russian, isn't she? It's all adding up."

"Indeed," Barker said, his eyes trained mercilessly on Julia. "Can I borrow you for a moment?"

Barker marched into the kitchen, leaving Julia to follow him like a mischievous child about to get a scolding. With the hair in her apron pocket, she felt like one. She glanced back into the café before heading through the beads. Sue and Dot watched nervously as they sipped champagne and Katie flicked through a bridal magazine, not realising how badly she had just landed Julia in it.

"Barker, I—"

"I'm an *ex*-detective inspector, Julia," he interjected, his hushed tone filled with disappointment. "And even if I weren't, I would still tell you how *reckless* it was of you to take a piece of DNA evidence from a crime scene!"

"Barker, let me just—"

"And without telling me?" Barker circled the stainless-steel island, his hands disappearing into his hair. "You can't tamper with this stuff. It's important. It could matter."

"Barker, it was—"

"A mistake?"

"A huge one." Julia pulled the hair out of her apron and tossed it onto the counter. "I didn't realise I was doing it until I did it. If it's Roxy's hair, I wanted to—"

"Protect her from the law?"

"Get an explanation first," Julia jumped in, her headache muddling her thoughts. "I wanted to hear it from her lips. If she killed Leah, I—"

"Let's not jump to conclusions." Barker's tone softened. "You don't look so good."

"I don't feel it." Julia sat on a stool, her hand

clamped against her forehead. "I didn't sleep a wink last night and a marching band has taken up residence in my head."

Barker walked to the sink and filled a glass with water. Reaching into his pocket, he pulled out a box of painkillers. He popped two out of their foil casing and slid them to Julia with a kind smile.

"I'll take the hair to the police," Julia said after tossing back the painkillers. "Just let this kick in first."

"The police?"

"It's evidence."

"It's too late for that." Barker sighed as he picked up the hair and held it up to the bright ceiling light. "If you admit to taking this, you could be charged with perverting the course of justice. You don't want to give them any reason to lock you up, especially since you've beaten them to the punch on half the crimes over the last year."

"But you're an ex-DI."

"Exactly." Barker tossed the hair onto the table. "*Ex*. There are no blurred lines anymore. It's them and us, and I'm not going to let you land yourself in it like that. If there's one hair, they'll find something. It's only a matter of time. DI Christie is—"

"DI?" Julia cut in. "I thought he was only a

detective sergeant?"

"John was promoted into my old job," Barker said. "He's welcome to it. I'm much more suited to the writing. He was gunning for that job before I came to Peridale, so I'm happy for him. Plus, it helps to have someone on the inside for finding out things before *The Peridale Post*."

"What happened to them and us?"

"It's no different than when you used to extract details from me." Barker sent her a quick wink. "John is hardly tight-lipped about the particulars anyway. I've just been to the station. He filled me in on everything that's happened so far. I told him it was for book research, and he didn't question me."

"He'll know you're telling me this."

"I know." Barker sat on the stool opposite Julia. "I think that's why he was so frank with the details. This one has them stumped. A woman vanishes from her house without a trace in the middle of cooking dinner and doesn't take a single thing with her? Signs of a struggle, and some blood, but not enough to kill someone."

"It wasn't?"

"Not even close. Forensics are testing it to see if they can get a match from the DNA they've gathered from Leah's things. Until then, they're treating this like a missing person's case."

*Missing person.*

It felt so informal and unimportant, and yet Julia knew it was so much more significant than that. An invisible clock ticked down in the back of her mind, and she knew she would soon start chasing the hands to uncover the truth before time ran out. She checked her phone, but Roxy had yet to respond.

"Do you know anything else?" Julia asked, hoping for another revelation. "Any sightings?"

"Nothing." Barker shook his head. "They're tracing Leah's credit cards and banking, but she left everything in the house, so it's unlikely they're going to find her that way. Last I heard, Christie was about to set up a door-to-door search to see if anyone saw anything. Until then, it's like she's vanished into thin air. It's going to be a tough one for us to crack."

"Us?"

"Them and us, remember." Barker reached across the table and took Julia's hands in his. "If I can get leads from Christie, I will, but right now we're one step ahead." Barker released one of Julia's hands and picked up the bag. "And besides, we have something they don't—and there's no easy way to pass this on without putting you in their bad books. You know what we have to do."

"Find Roxy?"

"Find Roxy," Barker echoed, nodding firmly. "Any idea where to start?"

# 6

L eaving Katie in charge of the quiet café, Julia and Barker set off in search of Roxy. They circled the village green, assessing the groups of families enjoying early afternoon picnics in the burning heat. Neither of them acknowledged it, but Julia knew they were searching the crowd for Leah or Roxy. A football from a children's game darted across the grass towards them, and Barker kicked it back, a smile pricking the corners of his lips.

"And the world keeps turning," Julia murmured as she rubbed her temples, the sweltering temperature the only thing distracting her from the dull pounding in her head. "Everything feels so normal even when it isn't."

"It is for them." Barker wrapped his arm around Julia's shoulders and gave her a reassuring squeeze. "I know you're thinking about the worst-case scenario, but thinking doesn't mean it's true."

"That Leah is dead?"

Barker didn't respond.

"And if Leah is dead, that Roxy might have been the one to kill her?"

Silence.

"I'm tired," she apologised. "I don't want either to be true, but I can't see any other alternatives right now."

Julia pulled her phone from her small handbag and called Roxy again. She shouldn't have been disappointed when it diverted straight to voicemail, but she was. She hung up without leaving another message; she had already said everything she could say.

Roxy lived with her girlfriend, Violet, in a small flat above a candle shop at the top of Mulberry Lane, three doors up from *Brooke's Bridal Boutique*. Seeing the dress shop twisted Julia's stomach into a tight knot. Brooke's son, Max, was smoking a cigarette outside the shop, one foot leaning against the old stone. He had a white bag from the pharmacy clutched in his free hand. She stopped in her tracks, her mouth going dry as she watched him.

"He knows what happened between Brooke and Leah," Julia said, nodding to the lanky, dark-haired boy. "He looked like he wanted to throttle Leah as much as his mother did when he realised who she was. I should go over and ask him what he—"

"Maybe we should stick to the task at hand." Barker nodded to the bright pink door leading up to Roxy's flat. "If the fight was as bad as you described, we don't want to cause round two. Your association with Leah might be enough for him to snap."

"But what if he knows something important?"

"What if he doesn't?"

Max finished his cigarette, stubbed it against the wall, and tossed it into the gutter. He glanced in Julia's direction, his eyes meeting hers. She waited for a flicker of recognition, but he gazed right through her before ducking into the shop. Julia wiped the gathering sweat from her forehead as she made a mental note to speak to either Max or Brooke to see how they slotted into the puzzle of Leah's past.

Abandoning the lure of the dress shop, Julia turned her attention to Roxy's flat door. It had been a dull grey before Roxy had moved in, but in typical Roxy fashion, she hadn't wanted anything ordinary, so she had painted it hot pink within an hour of having the keys. Julia had helped paint the rest of the flat, which was just as exuberantly themed. There was no doorbell to ring or knocker to bang, so Julia rapped on the wood with her knuckles. They waited for sounds of movement, but nothing came.

"This is eerily familiar," Barker said as he took his turn knocking on the door. "If she's not here, where could she—"

Feet pounded down the staircase behind the door, cutting Barker off midsentence. A chain rattled, and the lock clicked before the door swung open with force.

"Rox—Oh, hello, Julia." Violet didn't try to hide her disappointment at their presence, her thick Russian accent transforming the words to 'uh, hullo, Julia.'

"You haven't heard from her either?" Julia offered a sympathetic smile when she noticed bags similar to her own under Violet's sparkling blue eyes. "I was hoping she would be here."

"She is not." Violet glanced up and down the street

as she tucked her long, silver hair behind her ears. Despite her tired eyes, Violet was still as strikingly beautiful as ever. With her pearlescent skin and elongated, svelte figure, Julia had always suspected Violet had been a runway model in a previous life. "Would you like to come in? The place is a little bit of a mess, but you know what Roxy is like."

"We don't want to impose." Julia shook her head, sensing Violet's invitation had been out of politeness. "From the way you shot down those stairs, I'm going to assume you don't know Roxy's current whereabouts?"

"I do not." Violet exhaled, wrapping her arms around herself as though she was cold. "I haven't seen her since yesterday evening. She said she was going to confront Leah and she hasn't been back since. I told her it was a terrible idea, but when Roxy gets something in her head, there is nothing that can stop her. I am—" Violet's voice broke off, her steely expression faltering. She swallowed hard and stiffened her spine as though emotion was forbidden in such a situation. "I am very worried about her. She won't answer her phone. I have left many messages, but she hasn't called me back."

"I know that feeling." Julia checked her phone, but the only notification was another prompt to perform the system update she had been ignoring for the best part of two weeks. "Have you heard about Leah?"

"I have heard lots of things about *that* woman." Violet's emphasis on 'that' made Julia think Violet was about to spit again. "She is bad news."

"Have you heard that she has gone missing?"

"Missing?" Violet's brow crinkled. "Like a lost dog?"

Barker and Julia glanced at each other.

"It's a little more serious than that," Barker said, his tone carrying more authority than his retired status should have allowed. "We have reason to believe something has happened to Leah."

"Something?"

"Something bad," Julia said, the words almost jamming in her throat. "We found blood in her cottage."

"Oh." Violet's brow crinkled further, her arms curling more tightly around herself. "And you think Roxy had something to do with this?" Anyone who didn't know Violet might have thought her matter-of-fact tone was cold, but Julia knew better.

"We only want to talk to her," Barker said.

"I understand." Violet took a step back into the stairway, the bulb above the door casting a dark shadow across her hollow features. "I'm sorry. I cannot help you. Goodbye."

Before Julia could ask Violet what she knew about the friction between Roxy and Leah, the Russian beauty slammed the door. The lock clicked back into place, as did the chain. Julia considered knocking again, but she doubted Violet would grace them with a second appearance.

"Where to next?" Barker asked, rubbing his hands together as he looked up and down Mulberry Lane.

They walked to Roxy's mother's home, on the outskirts of the village. Unlike most people in Peridale, Imogen Carter didn't live in a cottage. Her 1930s art deco house was fronted with more angular windows than seemed possible, giving it an alien quality. It sat between two ordinary, centuries-old cottages, looking as out of place as a lemon in a bowl of tomatoes. In her youth, Julia had spent a lot of time in the Carter home, along with Johnny, Roxy, and Leah. Imogen had always been so warm and inviting to her daughter's school friends, so it was where they had naturally ended up on their weekends.

Imogen, who had become somewhat of a recluse since her eldest daughter, Rachel, was convicted of a double murder over a year ago, answered the door with eyes that clearly indicated she rarely saw natural daylight. The warm and bubbly personality Julia remembered had been replaced with a skittish shell of a woman.

"Roxy?" Imogen shook her head after they asked her the same question they had asked Violet. "Haven't seen her in days. Has something happened?"

Not wanting to unload even more chaos on Imogen, Julia and Barker left without filling her in on the details. On their walk back through the village, they dropped into the B&B, but Evelyn hadn't seen Roxy either, nor had Shirley at The Plough. Feeling defeated, they retreated to the café, which was as empty as Julia had left it.

"No luck?" Katie asked as she sipped a cappuccino, foam on her top lip.

"None." Julia grabbed her apron from the hook in the kitchen. "I'm beginning to think she's performed another disappearing act like she did when her sister decided to go on that killing spree."

"Didn't you suspect Roxy then, too?" Katie crinkled her nose. "Statistically, it means she *definitely* did it this time. You can't be suspected of murder twice and not have killed someone at least one of those times."

"It's still a missing person case," Barker reminded Katie with a stern look. "Let's not jump ahead of ourselves."

Despite Katie's innocence, her theory was logical. Roxy had been Julia's prime suspect when Gertrude Smith and her son, William, had been murdered. Gertrude had been blackmailing Roxy, threatening to out her relationship with Violet, who was Roxy's teaching assistant at the time. Scared of ruining Violet's life and career, Roxy had fled the village on the day of Gertrude's murder. Even though her timing had been exceptionally bad, Roxy had returned to the village the second she heard about the murder. Julia had felt like a fool for thinking her best friend could murder two people in cold blood, and she had vowed never to be so stupid again. She pulled the hair out of her pocket, wondering if she was re-treading that familiar path, but something felt different this time.

Julia was ripped from her memories when Barker's phone started ringing, but she didn't linger to see who was calling. As she gazed out her café window, Johnny ran past, crouched over as though chasing something. Not wanting to miss her opportunity to catch him, she darted for the door with her untied apron hanging around her neck.

"Johnny Watson!" Julia planted her hands on her hips. He bent down to pick up what appeared to be a can of soup. "Is your phone broken?"

"Julia. I—"

"Are you about to lie to me, Johnny?" Julia interrupted. "Your ears are turning bright red."

Johnny grazed his right ear with his free hand as he peered down at the soup label.

"This was the last can. Shilpa said someone came in and cleared her of all her chicken soup last night." He walked past Julia and picked up a plastic bag, which had a hole in the bottom. "I think she has started using cheaper bags." Johnny laughed awkwardly as he knotted the bottom of the bag. "She still had the nerve to charge me for it."

"Johnny..."

"I'm sorry." He fiddled with his glasses, his eyes fixed on the cobbled road. "I didn't know what to say to you. Seeing Leah brought up so much. I didn't want to relive the past."

"Have you heard?"

"Heard what?"

"Leah is missing."

Johnny's brows tensed, as he met Julia's gaze. As he fiddled with his glasses, the redness spread down his ears and to his neck.

"Oh." Johnny replied, not sounding shocked. "Since when?"

"Since last night."

Johnny rubbed his neck, looking up at the sky as though waiting for a house to drop on him. Julia folded her arms and stared, waiting for him to speak.

"I should really go." Johnny hooked his thumb over his shoulder. "I have things to do."

Julia grabbed Johnny's collar with both hands, yanking him towards her. She stared deep into his eyes, their noses almost touching.

"Listen to me, Johnny Watson." She tightened her grip. "I haven't slept, my head is banging, and it's hotter than the surface of the sun. Leah is missing, I can't find Roxy, and I still have no idea what is going on. I've known you since the first day of nursery. Far too long for you to be playing games with me. Tell me what happened twenty years ago. I *need* to know."

Johnny gulped as sweat dripped down his face. One drop rolled off the tip of his nose. If Julia were in her right mind, she would never have been so forceful with her old friend, but her right mind was nowhere to be found. He glanced at the group on the village green, eyes begging for help. Julia could sense them all watching, but she didn't break her stare.

"Leah ran off with my sister's fiancé on their wedding day," he finally spat out, words jumbling together. "She ruined my family's life."

Julia let go, startled that she hadn't known the jilted bride was Johnny's sister. She wracked her brain for Johnny's sister's name. "Heidi? I haven't seen her in years."

"She was hardly going to stick around here after being embarrassed like that, was she?" Johnny straightened his collar before wiping the sweat from his blotchy face. "She's my half-sister on my dad's side. We're not that close. She lives over in Riverswick, and her life hasn't been the same since Leah ruined it. Are you surprised I wasn't happy to see her?"

"I had no idea."

"I didn't tell anyone when it happened." Johnny leaned in and lowered his voice. "I didn't want to make things worse for my sister. People still heard rumours, but we did everything we could to protect Heidi."

"What does this have to do with Roxy?"

"Nothing." Johnny looked perplexed. "Her problem with Leah has nothing to do with my sister. Look. I really do need to go. I have a meeting with my editor. I have a feeling he's about to tell me they're making even more cuts to the newspaper." He paused and fiddled with his glasses. "If you ask me, you should just leave this alone. Anything connected to Leah is going to mess with your life, okay? I had nothing to do with it."

"I never said you did."

With that, Johnny left, leaving Julia confused as to why he would think she would consider him a suspect. The idea hadn't occurred before, but it certainly took pride of place in her thoughts now.

"Julia?" Barker appeared behind her in the café doorway. "Is everything okay?"

"The man Leah ran off with was Johnny's sister's fiancé." Julia looked at the staring faces on the green, embarrassed at the show she had put on. "That's one piece of the puzzle."

"It's a start." Barker tapped his phone against the palm of his hand. "That was DI Christie. They've found something."

Julia's heart dropped to the floor as the pounding in her head increased tenfold. Much as she wanted to ask what they had found, the words wouldn't come.

"It's not a body," he assured her at once, reaching for her hand. "They've found a bag of clothes dumped out in the field behind Leah's cottage. Do you have any idea what Leah was wearing yesterday?"

"A yellow blouse and jeans."

Barker nodded, the lack of surprise in his expression telling her he'd already known.

"They're running them through forensics to be sure." Barker ran his hand over his stubble. "There's one more thing. They were covered in blood."

"How much blood?"

"A lot."

Julia nodded, the news somehow unsurprising. Exhausted and confused, Julia walked into her café and headed into the kitchen with hopes that baking something would help clear her mind.

# 7

After almost burning down the kitchen while attempting to bake a chocolate cake, Katie insisted Julia go home. Julia resisted, but she knew she was in no fit state to serve her regulars.

Driving home, Julia slowly passed the circus surrounding Leah's cottage. DI Christie stood at the edge of the garden, watching the forensic team work. From the stubble on his jaw and the wrinkles in his suit, he looked like he had slept as much as Julia had.

Despite her drained state, Julia found herself hesitant to sleep. The details of the disappearance were swirling in her mind and she was sure they wouldn't leave her alone. She pulled out her notepad and sat in the armchair by the window. She only managed to write 'Leah stole Heidi's fiancé' before sleep claimed her.

She jolted awake hours later, just as the sun was giving out its last rays for the day. Rubbing her eyes, she looked down at the notepad in her lap. For a moment, her foggy mind allowed her to forget the chaos of the last few days, and she wondered what she was looking at. A quick glance at the white tent surrounding the cottage across the road jogged her memory.

After a hot shower and a cup of peppermint and liquorice tea, Julia knocked on the dining room door before entering. Barker was at his usual spot at the head of the table, his eyes and fingers glued to his laptop. Julia turned on the ceiling light as dusk claimed the room. A mess of papers covered the table. She had grown so used to Barker's novel writing burying the surface that it took her a moment to realise they were not his writing notes. Neat stacks of 'MISSING PERSON' posters filled the table, each with a colour photograph of Leah centred in the middle.

"What's all this?" Julia picked up one of the sheets. "Did Christie drop these off?"

"I made them." Barker nodded at the printer in the corner. "Had to run out to buy more ink halfway through. Found the picture on one of her online profiles. What do you think?"

Julia stared down at the smiling picture of Leah. The photo had been taken on a sunny day, and from her pretty cream dress and glass of champagne in her hand, she looked like she was at a wedding.

"What are we going to do with them?"

"Post them all over the village." Barker finished typing his sentence, punctuating it with one final stab before slapping the computer shut. "I've done the rounds on social media, too. If someone has seen Leah, we're going to hear about it. I've put my number on the poster."

Julia smiled her appreciation of Barker's willingness to be proactive. She wanted to feel as optimistic as he did, but she couldn't summon the energy.

"What if it's all too little too late?" She placed the poster back on its pile. "The struggle, the blood, the clothes—you know it's all pointing to one thing."

Barker drained the last of his coffee before standing

and pushing the chair under the table; she wondered how much caffeine he had consumed during his printing session.

"That's the obvious explanation." Barker picked up a shoulder bag and began stuffing it with posters. "But this isn't like anything I've seen before. If someone is going to spontaneously commit murder, why go to the trouble of moving the body? You're only making things harder for yourself by creating a path of evidence. That the forensic team are still combing over the cottage tells me they have yet to find anything substantial. If Leah had been murdered there, they'd know by now. We're not going to give up hope. Until we know for certain, we have to distribute these posters far and wide. The more eyes see these, the more likely we're going to get a phone call. Someone might have seen something without realising how important it was." Barker picked up a second empty bag and passed it to Julia. "Are you in?"

Julia didn't even have to think about it. She took the bag and filled it with the rest of the posters. Barker's enthusiasm was all she needed to shake her from the dark pit her mind had fallen into.

"Hope," Julia said as she slung the heavy bag over her shoulder. "If that's all I have to cling to, then I'm going to cling."

They headed out into the night with the posters, a stapler, and a roll of tape. They attacked every lamppost and flat surface they could find, wrapping the entire village like a Christmas present. Shilpa put one in the post office window, Evelyn took several to scatter around her B&B, Shirley let them put one on each table in The Plough, and all the shops still open on Mulberry Lane took one to hang up; they avoided *Brooke's Bridal Boutique*.

Julia and Barker split up when they reached the village green. Julia decided she was going to drop some in at the village hall, and Barker walked back to his car to cover the villages surrounding Peridale. The village hall was in the middle of a slimming club meeting, so she snuck in and pinned a couple to the notice board before taping others in the windows of the door. She then moved onto St. Peter's Church, encouraged by the lights shining through the stained-glass windows. Pulling open the heavy doors, Julia examined a table in the vestibule. It was covered with leaflets advertising the church's services and events. She rearranged them, making room for a small pile of posters.

"Hello?" Father David appeared in the doorway, a pile of tattered Bibles in his arms. "Oh, Julia! What a lovely surprise. To what do I owe the pleasure?"

Julia held out one of the posters. Father David carefully placed his burden of books on the table before looking over the sheet. He sighed as he peered over his glasses to read the details.

"What a terrible shame," he said solemnly, shaking his head and handing Julia the poster. "Please, leave as many as you can. I'll pass them around the congregation on Sunday. Is Leah a local woman? I'm afraid I don't recognise her."

"She used to be. Emily Burns was her mother."

"Of course." He snapped his fingers together. "Leah Burns. Forgive me for my slowness. I didn't quite recognise her. It must have been years since I last saw her. I had no idea she had returned to the village."

"Not many did." Julia paused, a question suddenly burning in her mind. "Can I ask you something, Father?"

"Always."

Father David motioned to two chairs pushed up against the wall underneath a notice board. Julia had known the ageing vicar for all her life. He had always been a comforting ray of light in the village. She didn't know anyone who had a bad word to say about him.

"I'm not a particularly religious woman," she

started, her tone apologetic. "I wouldn't say I was an atheist, I'm just not sure what I believe, so I apologise if I'm crossing the line asking for your advice, or, rather, God's advice."

"God doesn't judge those who have yet to find him." He offered a kind and sympathetic smile. "What's troubling you, my child?"

Julia looked down at the picture of Leah, unsure where to start.

"I was friends with Leah a long time ago."

"I remember."

"I always thought Leah was a kind person, but it seems others don't share that opinion. I'm beginning to wonder if I ever knew her at all. She did some terrible things before she left the village. Unforgivable things, judging by the reactions of the people she wronged. I'm struggling to come to terms with the idea that I could have been so wrong about someone I thought I knew."

Father David appeared to consider Julia's words for a moment. He then nodded and exhaled.

"People are complicated, Julia." He smiled again, his lined face filled with wisdom. "Nobody is free of sin. Not even Jesus Christ himself could have navigated life without making a mistake—we just didn't hear about them in the Bible because it wouldn't have made for good reading. Just because others share a different opinion of a person than you do, it doesn't mean your perception is wrong. People can have many sides, and good people can do bad things, but God is a forgiving being. If there was no chance for repentance, then what would be the point of life? If someone is truly sorry in their heart for their misdoings and they ask for forgiveness, God will pardon them. It's as simple as that. Individual acts don't define our paths for the rest of our lives. Our journeys are made up of our choices, good and bad. These choices may define us in the moment, but that doesn't mean they have to define our future." He pulled off his glasses and rubbed them on the edge of his black robes. "I don't know what Leah did, and I don't think it's my place to ask, but she has had to live with her decisions in the years since she left. Am I right in assuming you think her disappearance is somehow linked to the events of the past?"

"I think so."

"Then I will pray for her safe return." He rested his hands on hers. "And I will pray that your own struggle will reach some resolution. You're a kind and charitable woman, and whether you realise it or not, you *are* a child of God. He will look after you and guide you if you're willing to let him in."

"Thank you, Father."

Julia stood up handed him a chunk of the posters. She turned to leave, but a distant light through the darkness of the window caught her attention.

"Is that the school?" Julia asked, pointing to the light. "It's the summer holidays."

Father David looked over his glasses and squinted. He seemed as puzzled as Julia felt.

"I haven't noticed that light on before." He tapped his finger on his chin. "Perhaps they're preparing the school for the new term?"

"Maybe."

Julia left the church and squinted at the soft, glowing light. She almost ignored it, but a niggle in the back of her mind forced her to investigate. Crossing the church grounds, she hopped over the encircling stone wall, and made her way down the lane that led to St. Peter's Primary School. When she reached the end of the lane and pushed open the front gate, she realised that the light was coming from one room—the classroom Roxy taught in.

Julia hurried across the playground, peered through the window's blinds, and saw Roxy, pacing back and forth in front of a clean whiteboard. Julia wanted to let out a triumphant cheer, but she held back.

Instead, she gently knocked on the window, startling Roxy. The redhead squinted in Julia's direction. When she realised who had knocked on the window, her expression resembled that of a child who had been caught doing something naughty. A side door that led directly into the classroom opened, and Roxy appeared, her cheeks as red as her hair.

"I don't know whether I want to hug you or slap you right now," Julia said, her jaw tightening. "Damn you, Roxy Carter!"

"I wouldn't be angry if you did both." Roxy stepped to the side and swung open the door. "I suppose I should invite you in."

Julia marched into the brightly lit classroom. A whiteboard hung where the blackboard used to be, and the colourful displays on the walls were different, but everything else was as Julia remembered from her youth. The wooden tables looked as tatty as they had when she had been a student, although, from her taller viewpoint, everything seemed to have shrunk. The teacher's desk—Roxy's desk—was cluttered with chocolate bar wrappers and two empty bottles of wine.

"I forgot to hand in my keys for the side door before summer," Roxy explained, walking back to her desk. "Each classroom is on a separate alarm system."

"What are you doing here?" Julia cried, looming over Roxy. "I've been trying to call you!"

"I know." Roxy glanced at her phone, which was charging on the floor. "My phone must have died at some point yesterday, and I was too busy drinking wine and feeling sorry for myself to notice. I couldn't bring myself to listen to all your messages. You sounded so angry."

"I *am* angry!"

"I'm sorry," Roxy whined, her teeth biting into her bottom lip. "You know I'm a mess, Julia. I've always found it hard to face my problems head on. I went to see Leah yesterday to attempt it, but it all went belly up. As usual."

"I know."

"You do?"

"Violet told me." Julia sat at the tiny desk nearest the front, her behind barely fitting on the chair. "She's just as worried as I am."

"I've seen her messages." Roxy huffed. "English might not be her first language, but she can certainly get creative with her swear words when she needs to."

Roxy's attempt at laughter curdled at whatever she saw on Julia's face.

"I can't believe you're being so trivial about this!"

"About what?"

"*Everything!*"

"So, I shouldn't be here," Roxy replied, her brows dropping defiantly. "It's not like I've *killed* someone. It's not a crime to drink wine and eat chocolate. Well, maybe the trespassing part is a crime, but I've done nothing wrong."

"You have no idea what's going on, do you?"

Roxy frowned and shook her head.

"Leah is missing," Julia said, for what felt like the hundredth time that day. She pulled a poster out of her bag and tossed it onto Roxy's desk. "I went to speak to her last night, her cottage was a mess, and there was blood on her carpet. Nobody has seen her since, and her bloody clothes have turned up in a field."

Roxy looked over the poster, her lips trembling as she read what Barker had written. She leaned back in her chair and stared through the poster to the back of the room.

"I-I-I—"

"Did you kill her, Roxy?"

"*What?*"

"Did you kill Leah?"

"And again—*what?*" Roxy gazed at Julia as though she had just grown an extra head. "I can't *believe* you even need to ask me that!"

"I found one of your hairs at the cottage." Julia reached into her pocket and pulled out the crinkled plastic bag. "I took it before the police could find it. I've circled this village trying to look for you."

"I don't deny that I went to Leah's cottage," Roxy replied, barely looking at the hair. "In fact, I brought it up *before* you did. I thought you were angry because I'd disappeared, not because you thought I'd *killed* someone!"

Julia felt apprehensive about suspecting Roxy of murder for a second time. Roxy had never learned to lie. She was too brash and honest to fib convincingly, especially to Julia. They had always been able to see right through each other.

"When I went to see her, she was *very* much alive, and her cottage was intact." Roxy sat up straight and put the poster on the table. "After spending a day upset that she was back, I wanted to try and sort things out for the sake of my relationship with Violet. I didn't want what Leah did to me hanging over us for however long she was planning on sticking around. I went to confront her about what she was doing back here, and in true Leah fashion, she didn't want to talk about it. She wanted to pretend like the past didn't happen. I was angry, but even if you'd put a knife in my hand, I wasn't angry enough to *kill* her."

"And what did she do to you?" Julia asked. "I know what she did to Johnny, but he seems to think that had nothing to do with you."

"Then he thought wrong." Roxy's voice lowered. She rustled a piece of a foil chocolate wrapper between her fingers. "Heidi wasn't the only one who had her heart broken by what Leah did." Roxy inhaled deeply, and Julia could tell that whatever her friend was about to share was difficult to talk about. "Do you remember my seventeenth birthday party?"

"Vaguely." Julia nodded. "I seem to remember I ended up looking after you because you were blind drunk."

"That's because you're a good friend." Roxy smiled softly. "And you deserve better than a mess like me."

"Just get on with the story, eh, Roxy?" Julia injected some frivolity into her voice to relax her friend. "Your party?"

"Right." Roxy inhaled again as her eyes glazed over. "It was the weekend after my birthday. My mum had gone to visit an old friend in Scotland, so, naturally, I invited everyone I knew for a party. Rachel bought us those cans of cider, which was a mistake on her part, but she only did it because I begged her to. I started drinking, and I felt my whole teenaged existence crash down around me. I was sick of pretending."

"Pretending what?"

"That I wasn't a complete lesbian," Roxy said with a sparkle in her eyes. "It was a different time back then, wasn't it? I'd known that I liked girls for as long as I could remember, but the idea of coming out in 1995 terrified me. It's such a bizarre concept. 'Oh, by the way, not that it's any of your business, but I'm attracted to the same sex.' That night, for whatever reason, I felt like I was carrying a secret bigger than I could handle. We'd just got our exam results, and we were about to start college. My entire world was shifting around me. Being a teenager is hard enough without all that extra sexuality confusion." Roxy checked the bottles of wine, but they were both empty. "One can of cider got me drunk back then, and I think I drank four in the space of an hour. I needed to tell someone, and it would have been you if you'd walked into my bedroom at that moment, but I ended up telling Leah instead." She paused and ran her hands down her face. "I can't believe I'm telling you this. The only person I've told in twenty years is Violet, and that was only because I couldn't pretend I wasn't upset that Leah was back."

"What happened?"

"I was crying in my bedroom," Roxy continued, her finger circling the mouth of the bottle. "What's more dramatic than a teenager crying in their bedroom during their birthday party? Have you ever second-guessed your sexuality?"

"I've never put much thought into it."

"Most people never do, but if you're not the norm, you're conditioned to look at it like it's a problem. In an ideal world, it would be a non-issue, but we're not there yet. I spent my entire childhood trying to fit in. I had more boyfriends in my teens than anyone, remember? I buried my sexuality down so deep that usually I could convince myself it wasn't there. That night, though, it burst out of me. Leah heard me crying, and she came in. She made me tell her what was on my mind. I barely put up a fight. I just blurted it out before I could stop myself. I don't know what I expected to happen. I'd built it up so much in my mind, I was surprised when the ground didn't start shaking. Do you know how Leah reacted?"

Julia shook her head.

"She kissed me." Roxy's eyes darted to Julia's. "She didn't say a word, she just kissed me. My first kiss was with a girl I'd been friends with for as long as I could remember. I'd never even looked at her like that, but, at that moment, I felt like I wasn't alone. When she pulled away, I was so confused. She had a smile on her face that I've never forgotten. It was like she'd just won a prize, and she was trying to figure out what to do with it."

"And what did she do with you?" Julia asked, shocked at where their conversation had gone.

"She tortured me. For the next two years, she dangled it over me. She convinced me not to tell anyone about my sexuality or the kiss. She made all these vague promises about us being together one day, and I fell for them hook, line, and sinker. We never kissed again. We never so much as held hands. At first, I didn't realise what was going on. I was just a kid. I thought I'd fallen in love. It felt like love. But it wasn't—it was manipulation. She dragged it out until the end of college, and she made me swear to keep it secret. It was like a game to her, even though she was the only one playing it. We were both going to the same university to study teaching. And then she ran off with Johnny's sister's fiancé three weeks before we were due to move. No goodbye, no explanation. One day she was here, and then she wasn't. I didn't understand. I felt like my future had been ripped away from me. I was numb. It took me years to realise she'd never been in love with me. Do you have any idea why someone would do that to another person?"

Julia shook her head.

"Me neither," Roxy continued. "That's what upset me so much. I couldn't figure out what she gained from treating me like that. She scarred me so much, I vowed never to tell another person again. Can you imagine that? I denied myself love until I was thirty-six. *Thirty-six*, Julia. I spent almost two decades hiding something that huge about myself because Leah screwed me up."

"You could have told me," Julia said, wanting to reach out and grab Roxy.

"I know that *now*." Roxy smiled her appreciation. "But until you've kept a secret that long, you can't know what it's like. It gets harder to reveal every year. It became taboo. Things didn't change until I met Violet." Roxy's frown turned into a heart-warming smile. "We had a spark instantly. I'd spent so long denying that part of myself, I didn't notice Violet was even flirting with me until she told me afterwards how hard she'd been trying to get my attention. We ended up kissing at the Christmas party, and that's when I gave in and decided I wasn't going to hide anymore."

Roxy pushed her hands through her already-messy

hair. "Then, you know, all that mess with Gertrude happened, and it reminded me what Leah did. I felt like I was being forced into keeping a secret again, so I ran away, and my sister *murdered* people. Fast forward to now. You tell me Leah is back like I'm supposed to be glad about it—and then I see her, and I'm that confused teenager who doesn't understand why her friend is treating her the way Leah did."

"If I'd had any idea, I would—"

"Don't, Julia. You've done nothing wrong. I freaked out. I should have just told you, woman to woman, what happened, so you could understand my reaction. When I saw her last night, she refused to acknowledge anything had happened between us. She was convincing, too. I wondered if I'd just imagined the whole sorry affair. Except the feelings were as raw as ever, and I knew she was just continuing her same old game. I left in a huff, bought copious amounts of wine and chocolate from the shop, and then I came here. I stayed up drinking and crying until sunrise, and then I passed out at my desk. I only woke up a couple of hours ago. I admit, when I saw Violet's messages and heard some of your voicemails, I panicked and didn't want to face anything, so I just … stayed here. I had no idea anything else was happening." Roxy looked down at the poster. "What time did you go to see Leah?"

"About nine."

"I was there at seven." Roxy glanced at the clock. "We went around in circles for ten minutes at the most, and then I left."

"And nothing seemed strange to you?"

Roxy thought about it for a moment, her eyes suddenly widening.

"There was one thing." She nodded, her finger tapping on the desk. "She kept looking at the ceiling. It was like she was trying to get back to something more important, which made me feel even angrier, and I was sure I could hear someone snoring, too."

"Snoring?"

"It could have been a tractor driving down the lane."

"Do you think someone could have been up there?"

"Maybe. I don't have any reason to believe there wasn't." Roxy's eyes widened even further. "I thought maybe she had a boyfriend or a husband, or maybe even a kid."

"She came back alone."

"Oh." Roxy sat up straight. "Do you think whoever killed her was up there when I was downstairs?"

"We don't know if she's dead yet." Julia stood and grabbed the poster from the desk. "Hence me handing these out."

"Well, just don't expect me to help you. I care about you, and it's clear you care about finding Leah, but that's not my journey. I'm done with her. If she's dead, I'll be sorry it came to that, but I won't shed another tear over her." Roxy's phone vibrated against the floor, and Roxy glanced down at it. "Violet's calling me. I really should go home, shouldn't I?"

"You should."

"I'm sorry, Julia."

"You don't have to apologise. I've decided that I'd rather hug you than slap you."

They hugged it out in front of the whiteboard. Julia absorbed Roxy's angst and pain, and it made her wish she had noticed what was going on all those years ago, so she could have helped when it mattered. To find out that she had missed something so crucial in Roxy's life made her feel like she had failed her friend.

After helping Roxy hide the evidence of her out-of-hours school lock-in, Julia delivered her to the pink-doored flat on Mulberry Lane. Leaving Roxy to face Violet alone—some things didn't need an audience—Julia made her way home. Barker hadn't returned from his drive, and she was glad she could have some time with her thoughts. After stapling one last poster to a tree on the lane outside her cottage, Julia unlocked the door and retreated into the dark hallway.

Under her feet, something rustled on the doormat. Turning on the hallway lamp illuminated a manila envelope. Julia picked it up and turned it over. A message made from neat, cut-out newspaper headline letters greeted her:

**ThErE's MoRE tO thE StoRY ThaN YoU KNOw!**

Julia ripped open the envelope and pulled out a single sheet of paper. It appeared to be a newspaper article pulled from *The Peridale Post*'s digital archive. Julia walked into her dark sitting room, turned on the lamps, and perched on the sofa next to Mowgli before reading:

*June 23rd, 1995*

## NOT GUILTY! ACCUSED TEACHER VINDICATED BY JUDGE!

After a lengthy investigation and trial, a jury at Cheltenham Magistrates' Court found local high school drama teacher, Gary Williams, 41 (pictured below), not guilty of sexually assaulting a pupil. The pupil, who cannot be legally named because of their age, claimed Mr Williams attempted to kiss them after months of emotional grooming. Williams, who has always vehemently denied the charges as nothing more than the 'delusions of a manipulative fantasist teenage girl', left the court with his wife, Carol Williams, by his side. Williams, a free man, was in good spirits. Judge Byron condemned the 'baseless' and 'reckless' accusations in his closing address, going on to warn others to 'think twice before attempting to destroy a person's career with malicious lies.' Gary Williams, who taught at The Hollins High School, was relieved of his position at the beginning of the investigation. He told the press he was 'hopeful' the school would 'reconsider their decision', but with...

Julia turned the paper over, but the article didn't continue on the other side. Instead, she found more cut-out letters:

## WhO DO U tHInk ThIS is ABOut???

While she'd been reading, Julia had already decided the

pupil who couldn't be 'legally named because of their age' must have been Leah. She vividly remembered the trial, which had happened in her final year at high school, but nobody had ever been able to figure out the accuser's identity, because of their anonymity. Julia had never suspected the accuser could have been Leah, but after what she had heard from Roxy, she no longer doubted that she knew absolutely nothing about the woman she had once claimed as a friend.

"What have I got myself into this time, Mowgli?" Julia sank into the sofa and tossed the envelope onto the table before tickling her cat's head. "How could I have been so wrong about someone?"

# 8

"A liar, a manipulator, *and* a cheater!" Dot exclaimed, waving her hands dramatically in the air. "I wouldn't be surprised if she was a thief and a murderer too!"

Dot passed the article to Katie, who read it over while slurping mouthfuls of Dot's secret recipe stew. Julia ladled another serving into her bowl. News of Leah's disappearance had finally spread around Peridale, no doubt thanks to Barker's posters. Whenever anything exciting happened in the village, the café became the official hub for gossip and speculation, resulting in a hectic day. Julia had heard dozens of wild theories about what could have happened to Leah, but her favourite was Evelyn claiming that she'd had a vision of Leah beaming up to an alien spaceship.

When Dot had insisted that Julia have dinner at her cottage to discuss wedding planning, Julia had been glad of the offer to do something away from the case. As it turned out, they had spoken of little else.

"I remember the trial," Sue said, dunking a bread roll into her gravy rich stew. "Gran tried to convince me to go to another school."

"Of course, I did." Dot shifted in her seat with a proud nod. "And I'd do it again. It made me wonder what other nefarious characters were lurking in those classrooms!"

"He was cleared," Julia reminded her. "The jury reached a unanimous verdict."

Julia and Barker had spent most of the previous night researching the trial. Thanks to *The Peridale Post* digitising their records, they had managed to piece together a timeline of the case. It had dragged out for months. The only thing they hadn't been able to confirm was if the accuser was Leah. Barker had attempted to call in a favour at the station to get the information, but that was one request too far.

"Well, there was no Mr Williams at Hollins when I was there." Sue shrugged before picking up another bread roll. "My drama teacher was Mrs Osbourne. She was such a hippie. Wouldn't wear shoes in the classroom and she had the ugliest hairy feet."

"What was Mr Williams like?" Katie asked. "I didn't go to the same school as you two."

"That's because you were privately educated with all that Wellington money." Dot rolled her eyes. "Not that it made much difference with you, dear."

Katie passed the article back to Julia. The black and white picture showed Gary Williams with his wife in front of the court. He wore a black suit and a look of relief. Even though the picture was grainy, it showed how handsome he was. His black hair was slicked back from a face composed of solid Viking angles.

"He was the teacher everyone fancied." Julia made circles in the stew with her spoon. "Most girls had a crush on him. He was funny, and he wasn't afraid to look silly. He was theatrical and eccentric. He was the type of teacher you wished taught every subject because he was so engaging."

"And Leah threw herself at him, and then spat her

dummy out of the pram when he rejected her!" Dot exclaimed, stabbing her finger on the table. "Teenaged girls never fail to surprise me. Nobody in this village believed he did what the girl claimed. Not a soul! We all saw through it, and so did the jury, but mud sticks around here. Poor man must have moved away. She ruined his life." Dot dropped her spoon and pushed the bowl away before picking up a stack of magazines and dropping them on the table. "Enough of this humdrum! We have a wedding to plan, and time is ticking, missing wedding planner or not."

Katie and Sue let out identical squeals of delight. The only person not excited about wedding planning was Julia. She had barely given the impending wedding a second thought since the incident at the dress shop.

"I wonder who sent this," Julia said as she touched the cut-up letters stuck on the envelope, unable to change the subject. "I spent all night wracking my brain, trying to understand why someone would want me to know this information."

"It's like something out of a film," Dot said. "It's almost cliché."

"It feels like a prop." Julia stared at the neat, perfectly-glued letters. "Someone wanted me to know this, but they didn't want me to know who they were.

Why?"

"Misdirection?" Dot suggested.

"A clue?" added Sue.

"Or the killer sent it!" Katie exclaimed. "Well, not 'the killer' because we don't know if she's dead, but maybe they want you to know why they did what they did, whatever it is."

Julia stared at the letters, hoping they would rearrange themselves to give her a clue. Something within her mind shifted, shining new light on the article; she felt like a clown for not figuring it out sooner.

"It *is* cliché." Julia scooped up the article. "A manila envelope, a printed page from *The Peridale Post*, perfectly cut-out newspaper pieces glued down to expose Leah without actually mentioning her. It's too clean and perfect, like someone is playing the role of a villain. It's so obvious! I need to go. Thanks for the stew, Gran."

"But the wedding planning!" Katie cried. "We were supposed to be looking at dresses."

"Another time! Got to go."


Johnny rented a tiny one-bedroom cottage on a remote lane leading out of Peridale. Most villagers refused to acknowledge that the area belonged to the village, but Johnny always made sure to mention that his postcode put him within Peridale's borders. It was the epitome of a single man's home, which might have felt a little sad for anyone else nearing their forties, but the miniscule building suited Johnny.

Julia climbed out of her car, the envelope containing the article crammed under her arm. She stormed past the gate hanging off its hinges and straight to the front door, glad when she saw movement and lights through the closed blinds. She knocked and waited for Johnny to answer.

When he did, wearing a matching set of bug-eyed-alien-print pyjamas and carrying a pot of microwave noodles in one hand, his gaze immediately dropped to the envelope. His face reddened before he blurted, "I've never seen that before."

"I never asked if you had." Julia slapped the envelope against his chest. "Can I come in?"

Without waiting for a response, Julia pushed past Johnny. His cottage, which had once been an outhouse for farm workers, consisted of two rooms. The sitting room, bedroom, and kitchen were all crammed into one, with a tiny bathroom in the other. The ceilings were low and beamed, and the wonky walls were filled with shelves of DVDs and boxed action figures. It looked more like a teenager's bedsit than a fully-grown man's home. In typical Johnny fashion, everything was immaculately neat and clean, which made the crunched-up newspaper clippings poking out of the kitchen bin even more obvious. Julia plucked one out, not surprised to see impeccably cut letters missing from the headlines.

"It looks like someone is stealing your letters." Julia peered through the holes at Johnny. "Care to explain?"

"Was it really that obvious?"

"I'm embarrassed to admit I had to sleep on it before I realised you were the only person who could be this obvious." Julia screwed up the newspaper and tossed it back into the bin. "I'll give you points for effort though. You painted a convincing picture."

"It's all true!"

"I know." Julia perched on Johnny's plump leather sofa. It squeaked under her weight as though it had never been used. "I conducted my own research. Why didn't you tell me? You could have called or sent a text. Or, better yet, you could have mentioned it when I saw you chasing soup cans. Why play games with me, Johnny? That's not your style."

Johnny sat next to her, the tight leather creaking.

He placed his pot of noodles next to his laptop on the shiny glass coffee table before dropping his face into his hands. Julia thought he was about to start sobbing, but he exhaled and dragged his fingers down his face, instead.

"I wanted to throw you off the scent."

"What scent?"

"*My* scent." Johnny's ears burned bright red. "I knew I'd be one of your suspects. You're not stupid."

"You weren't a suspect until you just said that." Julia searched her old friend's face. "What's going on? Is there something you're not telling me?"

Johnny didn't need to speak for her to know there was more to his story.

"There's nothing else."

"You're as good a liar as Roxy, Johnny," Julia said softly. "And you don't make a good villain. You're too sweet. Why would I suspect you?"

He paused again, the silence growing uncomfortable as the sofa groaned underneath them.

"Because of what Leah did to my sister. It's the obvious motive for wanting to hurt Leah. I didn't want you to think my sister or I had anything to do with it."

"Did you?" Julia asked, before quickly adding, "I have to ask."

"No."

"Then I believe you." Julia rested her hand on his knee. "You're my friend, Johnny. I just want to get to the bottom of this mess, so we can all get back to normal."

"There is no normal when Leah's around." Johnny glanced at the envelope. "You read the article. You know what she did to Mr Williams. She ruined his life."

"How did you find out it was her?"

"I work for a newspaper, Julia. It's our job to know." Johnny tried not to look impressed with himself, but he was as bad at concealing his emotions as he was at lying. "I started working for *The Peridale Post* around the time Heidi was ditched. I mentioned something to one of the guys at the paper and Leah's name rang a bell. They had it on record that Leah was the student who accused Mr Williams. Someone from the jury leaked it, but they couldn't legally print it because she was a minor, regardless of what she did. By the time she turned eighteen, there was no point in the paper exposing her like that. People had moved on."

"How do you think this is connected to what happened to Leah?" Julia asked. "Do you think Mr Williams had something to do with her disappearance?"

"I don't know what happened to him," Johnny admitted. "But you know who his daughter is, don't you? She runs that bridal shop on Mulberry Lane."

"Brooke?"

Johnny nodded.

Julia felt like a mental door had been blasted open. Suddenly, one of the most bizarre events of the last few days, the fight at the bridal shop, made perfect sense. She had just needed one tiny piece of information.

"No wonder Brooke reacted like she did when she saw Leah," Julia thought aloud, her finger tapping against her chin. "Leah tried to ruin Brooke's father's life, and then casually turns up to help me buy a wedding dress twenty years later."

"Motive enough for anyone," Johnny said, a little too eagerly. "So, does that rule Heidi and me out?"

"I'd need to speak to Heidi first."

"She was here with me when Leah vanished." Johnny jumped in, his cheeks flushing. "All night. We were watching movies."

Julia nodded. She knew Johnny was lying to protect his sister, but she decided not to push it. Even if he knew Heidi was behind Leah's disappearance, he wouldn't hand her over without a fight. For the time being, Julia had decided not to put him in that position;

he had given her plenty of new information.

"So, you're going to look into the Mr Williams side of things?" Johnny asked as he walked her to the door. "I think it's a good lead."

"I'll keep my ear to the ground." Julia opened the door, leaving behind Johnny's arts and crafts newspaper project. She pulled her keys from her bag, but paused before he closed the door behind her, something else springing to mind. "Your sister's ex-fiancé. Who is he?"

"Craig Wright," Johnny replied, his tone bitter. "I blame him as much as Leah, if not more. He's not shown his face around here since his marriage to Leah fell apart."

"Do you know where he is now?"

"Last I heard, he was living out at the Fern Moore Estate." Johnny gave Julia a puzzled look as he clung to the wooden door. "You're not going to go looking for him, are you?"

"I was just curious." Julia smiled through her lie. "Goodnight, Johnny. Please don't post anything more through my door. You have my phone number."

Before retreating into his cottage to finish his cold noodles, Johnny promised he wouldn't. Julia waited until she reached her car before pulling out her phone.

"Barker? How soon can you get to the Fern Moore

Estate?"

# 9

Much like Johnny's cottage, Fern Moore was technically part of Peridale. Villagers, however, denied any claim to the troubled housing estate that sheltered hundreds of low-income families. Most people avoided the place thanks to its reputation for unsavoury characters and criminal behaviour. Julia was amongst those who avoided the estate. She had been conditioned as a child to stay far away, and that conditioning had carried through to adulthood. In the handful of times she had visited, it had lived up to its unsavoury reputation.

The estate was composed of two towering, utilitarian blocks, each housing numerous cramped, tiny flats. Julia pulled up in a small car park facing the central concrete courtyard. The courtyard was a focal point for the estate, but unlike the pristinely manicured village green outside Julia's café, Fern Moore housed an out-of-date and graffiti-covered children's park. Groups of youths cluttered the darkened courtyard, cigarette smoke rising from them like plumes from a factory.

Dim streetlamps circled the courtyard, some flickering and others not working at all. Julia had parked underneath one of the few working lamps. The bright yellow light illuminated her vintage car, catching the suspicious eyes of more than a couple of the people milling around in the warm evening. She killed the engine and pulled out the keys, wondering what to do. She peered around for Barker's car, but he had yet to reach the estate. One of the groups, which consisted of four shirtless young men and one scantily-clad girl, made their way to her car, sneers and smirks on their faces. One of the lads drained a can of beer, crunched it between his hands, and tossed it in Julia's direction.

It bounced off her precious Ford Anglia's hood before rattling to the ground. The group let out a roar of laughter.

She considered locking herself in the car, but she knew the action would show her hand. She was not going to let them see how scared she was. After a deep breath, she climbed out and locked the door. The gang members folded their arms. She peered down at her vintage summer dress, knowing she should have swung by her cottage to change. She reeked of Peridale. The Fern Moore residents kept themselves to themselves, as did Peridale villagers; the two rarely met. There was an unspoken line in the sand that was not to be crossed. When someone dared cross it, the friction between the two sides was never more obvious.

Billy came to mind as Julia stared at the gang. Fern Moore had been his home before he crashed into Peridale, stealing Jessie's heart along the way. He had since turned his life around and now ran a builder's yard with Jessie's brother, Alfie. His petty criminal past was behind him, and he had surprised everyone by showing that he was a sweet boy under the prickly exterior. As she walked towards the group, she tried to imagine they were a pack of Billys.

"Good evening," she said, dropping her keys into

her handbag. "I was wondering if you might be able to help me."

"Need directions to the castle, princess?" one of the boys called, his voice far grittier than it should have been for someone his age. "Peridale's that way." He pointed to the road before spitting on the ground. "Get lost, alright?"

Julia clutched her bag and stiffened her spine. She should have expected such a reaction.

"I'm looking for someone," she continued, resolved not to give in so easily. "A man by the name of Craig Wright. I heard he lives here."

"So what?" the same guy said again, giving Julia the impression he was the elected leader. "Why should we tell you anything?"

"Make it worth our while." The girl stepped forward, nodding at Julia's bag. "Women like you probably have a few coins to spare."

Julia clutched her bag even tighter and took a step back. Looking around the courtyard, she found most of the gangs were now staring in her direction. She had wandered into the lion's den with a bloody steak strapped to her chest. She stole a glance at her car. Could she unlock it, climb inside, start the engine, and drive away before they closed in? She doubted it.

"First, I want to know that Craig Wright lives here." Julia poked up her chin and gritted her jaw. "Then, we can discuss bribes."

The group looked amongst themselves, snickering and shaking their heads at the Peridale woman brave enough to stand her ground. They were able to communicate with each other without saying a word. Julia felt her fate as a sleuth hanging in their hands.

"Yeah, he lives here," the leader said, stepping into the glow of the streetlamp. His skin was pock-marked, his exposed chest was lean, and his hair was spiked up with gloopy gel. He couldn't have been any older than twenty. "What do you want with a saddo like him?"

"He's an old friend," she lied.

"You need better friends," the girl said, also stepping into the light. "Cough up, and we'll tell you where he lives."

Julia looked around for Barker again, but his car was still nowhere to be seen. She carefully unclipped her bag and retrieved her purse. She had a little under £100 in notes, but she made sure not to show them off. She plucked out a crisp £20 note and handed it out. When they laughed, she pulled out a second. The leader snatched them out of her hand and stuffed the money into his pocket.

"104," he said, jerking his head to the first block. "Top floor."

Without any fuss or drama, the gang turned their backs on Julia and walked away, no doubt off to find something to spend their winnings on. She finally exhaled, her breath trembling as adrenaline rushed through her system. She hid her purse with shaky hands before word spread that she was offering handouts. When she turned back to her car, headlights blinded her as Barker pulled into the space next to hers.

"I told you to wait in the car." Barker slammed his door and hurried over, locking his vehicle with a click of his key over his shoulder. "Are you okay? Has something happened?"

"I'm not a damsel in distress, Barker." She forced the wobble out of her voice. "Everything is fine. I went ahead and uncovered some intel while you were driving under the speed limit. Craig lives in 104."

"How did you unearth that?"

"I have my ways."

They walked around the abandoned playpark to the stairwell where the lad had pointed. Julia told Barker everything Johnny had revealed as they walked. The lift had an 'OUT OF ORDER' sticker on it that was so faded it looked as old as the building. The concrete stairwell was colourfully graffiti-covered and musky smelling, so they didn't linger on their climb to the top floor. The exposed walkway in front of the flats was filled with litter and cigarette butts. Flat 104 sat in the middle of the top row. Its curtains were drawn behind the cracked, meshed window. A flickering TV burned through the darkness, hinting that someone was home.

"How do we know this is the right place?" Barker asked as they positioned themselves in front of the door. "Your sources could be playing a trick on you."

"Well, we'll find out, won't we?" Julia knocked and stepped back. "If this isn't Craig, we'll apologise and leave."

The noise from the TV paused, and the flickering stopped. Someone shuffled, but the door didn't immediately open.

"Who is it?" A gruff male voice barked through the door. "If Cameron has sent you, you can repeat what I already told him. I don't have the money yet, so just leave me alone, okay?"

"We're not with Cameron," Julia called back through the wood. "Craig? Craig Wright?"

There was a long pause. The man sounded as though he was shuffling towards the door.

"Who wants to know?" he called again, his voice closer. "Who sent you?"

"No one sent us." Barker took over. "We wanted to ask you some questions about someone you used to know."

"Who?"

"Leah Burns."

The silence that followed dragged out for an age, and Julia wondered if he had left via another exit. Just when she was about to knock again, the door opened a crack, secured by a chain. A tired-looking man stared at them, the heavy creases under his eyes hinting at years of sleepless nights. At least four days' worth of stubble speckled his chin and jaw, and the shiny texture of his thinning hair hinted that it had been as long since he had last showered. He wore a stained white vest that hung off his frame. Gaunt as he was, he had a pot belly only years of drinking could create.

"Craig?" Julia asked softly, stepping closer. "My name is Julia. We're here to talk to you about Leah."

"Are you police?" His eyes darted between them. "I have nothing to say about her."

"We're not the police," Julia said before Barker slipped into his old role. "I'm an old friend of Leah's." Julia hesitated, the role of 'old friend' no longer sitting comfortably. "I went to school with her. I just wanted to ask you a few questions."

"Why?" he demanded.

"Because she's missing," Barker said bluntly.

The door slammed shut, and the chain rattled before Craig opened the door fully. He stepped to the side and ushered them in before glancing up and down the walkway. He slammed the door and motioned for them to sit on the sofa.

Even in the hazy glow of the TV, Julia saw that every inch of Craig's flat was cluttered. Every surface was filled with books, DVDs, empty cups, and rubbish. The sofa was swathed in patterned blankets, and the coffee table was covered in piles of magazines and newspapers. Julia and Barker perched on the edge of the sofa, and stared at the TV, which was paused on a frame of Bruce Willis shuffling through a vent with a cigarette lighter.

"*Die Hard*," Barker said, nodding at the screen. "Good taste."

Craig hovered, chewing his nails. A meowing ginger cat appeared, and he scooped it up. It snuggled against his chest and purred as he stroked its back.

"Leah's missing?" he asked, sitting in an armchair next to an overwhelmingly filled bookcase. "Since when?"

"Two days ago."

The cat wriggled free and jumped onto the sofa arm. It sauntered across the back, sniffing curiously at the guests. Julia reached out and tickled under the cat's chin, which it took as an invitation to crawl onto her lap.

"He's not shy," Julia remarked as he stroked the cat's fur. "What's his name?"

"Rocky," he replied, his brow tense as he watched her pet the cat. "What are you doing here?"

"We already told you that—"

"Leah is missing," he interrupted sharply. "Yeah. I heard that bit. But what are you doing *here*? What does this have to do with me?"

Julia hadn't known what to expect, but considering everyone else's reactions surrounding Leah, she was not surprised to hear the hostile bite in his tone. He continued to stare at Rocky, perched on the armchair like he was a visitor in his own home.

"You're her ex-husband, so we thought—"

"That I'd know where Leah was?" He laughed bitterly. "I haven't seen the woman since she divorced me seventeen years ago. What's she doing back in Peridale anyway?"

"We never said she was back in Peridale," Julia said, squinting at him.

"Well, I just assumed!" he cried. "Don't play those tricks on me, lady. Are you sure you're not police? You said you went to school with her, so it's obvious she came back. She went to school in Peridale."

"Her mother died," Barker said. "She moved into the old house."

"Emily?" Craig asked, one brow arching. "Never met the woman. She wasn't too keen on coming to the wedding after we fled Peridale together." He paused, his expression softening. "Worst mistake of my life."

Julia assessed Craig as he appeared to slip back into his memories. He was a ghost of a man, clearly broken by years of struggle.

"Maybe you could tell us about your marriage to Leah?" Julia prompted. "Any information could help."

"It's ancient history." He hesitated, pursing his lips as though considering whether to divulge his story. "Rocky never likes strangers."

"I have a cat." Julia pulled her phone from her bag and showed him the wallpaper picture. "Mowgli. He's a Maine Coon."

"He's adorable." Craig smiled at the picture. "I've always loved cats. I should have known things were doomed with Leah when she wouldn't let me get one. If I'd asked that simple question before we ran off, it would have saved years of pain." He exhaled. "I was twenty-three, and Leah was eighteen. She came into my life at a time when I needed a distraction. Heidi was my high-school girlfriend. We beat the odds and made it through college and university together. I proposed because everyone told me that was the next step. I wasn't ready to get married and have kids. Settling down isn't for twenty-three-year-olds. It never lasts at that age.

"Heidi said yes to my proposal. She dove into the wedding planning like it was her full-time job. It cost me a fortune. Her family barely put anything towards the wedding. They never liked me. They always thought she was too good for me. Fern Moore people don't match you Peridale folk." Craig paused and looked them up and down. "You don't like us."

"Our daughter's boyfriend is from here," Barker said, grit in his voice. "Don't make wild assumptions. We're not here to judge your background."

"Then you're the exception." Evidently, Craig was not going to back down. "You probably weren't born in the village if you think like that." Barker shifted in his seat and nodded. "The wedding was coming at us like a steam train. I couldn't get off. I'd chained myself to a future I wasn't sure I wanted. And then, Leah exploded into my life like a firework."

Craig paused, looking into the distance as if seeing the memories playing there all over again. "We used to have a corner shop on the estate, but it closed years ago. Back then, I was doing every hour there I could to pay for the wedding. Then, one day out of the blue, this Peridale girl came in. I thought she was lost, but it's like she came to seek me out. I wasn't looking for anything, but Leah was relentless. She came in every day, flirting like it was her job. I tried to resist her, and I should have, but I was twenty-three and stupid. I ignored my instincts, and I fell in love with her. I didn't want to hurt Heidi, but I did. She went through something no woman should have to go through, and I did it to her."

He stopped talking. His eyes shone damp with unshed tears. As if Rocky could sense Craig's sadness, he crawled from Julia's lap and settled in his master's.

"The affair with Leah went on for three months," Craig continued, gulping down his emotions. "I called it off a week before the wedding. I told Leah it was over, and I couldn't see her anymore because I was marrying Heidi and that was that. I thought she got the message, but she turned up at my flat on the morning of the wedding. She gave me a get out of jail free card, and I took it. I packed a bag, and we went straight to the train station. We jumped on the first train without looking at the destination. We avoided the conductor to the end of the line. We ended up going north, to a town called Burnley. The rent was cheap, and jobs were going. I don't know what she was running away from, but we were running together. She didn't care about the danger. I think she enjoyed being a saboteur. The irony is, I ended up in the exact same situation I'd been trying to run from. We worked our behinds off to pay for a tiny flat. We married at the register office one afternoon because it felt like the right thing to do."

"How long did it last?" Julia asked.

"Seven months." Craig forced a laugh and shook his head. "She didn't announce she was leaving, she just went. I didn't hear from her until her lawyer sent me a letter about divorcing. I didn't put up a fight, I just went along with it. It bankrupted me. I came back here because I didn't know where else to go. I tried to talk to Heidi, if only to apologise, but she didn't want to hear it. I don't know if things would have worked with Heidi if Leah had never come into the shop that day, but I like to pretend they would have. Who knows what would have happened? Heidi deserved better than me, and I hope she's found it. Have you seen her recently?"

Julia shook her head. She decided not to tell Craig that Heidi, according to Johnny, had been living under a cloud, unmarried and humiliated ever since.

"Can I be honest with you?" he asked as Rocky jumped off his lap. Julia and Barker nodded. "I don't care what's happened to Leah. She was toxic then, and I don't imagine she ever changed. When I got back, I heard a rumour that she lied about some teacher kissing her and she ruined his life too. People like that don't have any goodness in their hearts—they just pretend they do to manipulate people." He stood up and yawned. "If you don't mind, I'd like to get back to my film. I can't help you."

Julia and Barker didn't try to stick around. They left the messy flat and the sad wreck of Craig Wright behind them. Silently, they walked back to the stairway, deep in their thoughts.

"Did you believe him?" Barker asked when he reached his car.

"Did you?"

"I believe Leah hurt him."

"He wasn't blameless in all of that." Julia pulled her keys from her bag and unlocked her car. "It takes two to tango. I don't know. I wanted to believe him, but something was off."

"I'm glad it's not just me then." Barker opened his door and pulled the bag of posters from the passenger seat. "I'm going to put some of these up before I head off. I haven't had any calls yet, but who knows?"

Barker looped the bag over his shoulder at the same moment his phone beeped in his pocket. Pulling it out, he stared at the screen, his eyes scrunching as he read the message.

"They've arrested Roxy," Barker said gravely. "There must have been a second hair after all."

# 10

J ulia woke with a fire in her belly the next morning. Roxy's arrest had made her even more determined to get to the bottom of the case. She had no doubt the police were jumping to the same wrong conclusion she had.

On her return from Fern Moore, Julia had filled half a notepad, piecing together the story of Leah's past. All the grisly details seemed even worse on paper, but Julia had decided to be objective in her search for the truth; Roxy was now her focus.

The timeline in her notes started in late 1994 with Leah accusing Gary Williams. In mid-1995, Gary was found not guilty. Later in 1995, it moved onto Roxy's confession to Leah, which resulted in Leah's game for two years, ending in the summer of 1997 when Leah ran off with Craig. According to Craig's claim that he hadn't seen her for seventeen years, which Julia assumed was at the hearing for their divorce, their relationship had ended sometime before 2001. She added in a second marriage somewhere between 2001 and 2009 because Leah said she had entered her thirties with two divorces under her belt. Between 2009 and 2018 she had Leah planning weddings, and the timeline finished with Leah returning to, and then vanishing from, Peridale.

Deciding to tackle what she hoped would be the easiest gap to fill in her notes, Julia closed the café an hour early and gathered Katie, Sue, and Dot for an impromptu dress shopping trip. They were surprised she was so keen to look at dresses again, and even more surprised when she suggested they revisit *Brooke's Bridal Boutique*.

"She's crazy!" Dot cried as they pulled up in front of the shop on Mulberry Lane. "She's going to attack us the second we walk through the door."

"There are other shops." Sue checked her watch. "If we hurry we can catch the one in Riverswick before they close for the day. I drove past their window display yesterday after I took the twins swimming. They have some really gorgeous dresses."

"I want to shop locally," Julia insisted, locking her car after they all climbed out. "They have nice dresses here. I'm sure everything will be fine. *We* didn't do anything wrong."

Julia was not sure at all; in fact, she was almost certain they would be thrown out and banned for life on sight, but she had a secret weapon up her sleeve that rarely failed to win people over. She opened the small paper bag and peered at the two pieces of leftover lemon drizzle cake she had packaged up for Brooke and Max.

Taking the lead, Julia pushed on the door and greeted Brooke with a smile. She was behind her desk, writing in a large, leather book. It took Brooke a moment to recognise Julia.

"*No!*" Brooke cried, throwing her pen on the desk as she darted up. "I'm not serving you."

It was the reaction Julia had expected.

"We came to apologise." Julia offered the bag of

cakes and placed them on the desk, careful not to get within grabbing distance. "We had no idea about Leah's connection to your family, and if we had, we never would have been so irresponsible as to bring her here."

Brooke peered into the bag with narrowed eyes, her thin lips tightening. If she appreciated the gesture, it was hard to tell; her sharp features were impossible to read.

"And besides," Dot exclaimed, stepping forward, "the woman is missing. We didn't even know her that well, did we, girls?"

"No," Katie and Sue chimed in.

"I honestly had no idea," Julia repeated as she searched Brooke's eyes for forgiveness. "I don't blame you for your reaction. I didn't know Leah as well as I thought."

Brooke's expression briefly softened before she stiffened and pulled down the edges of her suit jacket. After what felt like a lifetime of consideration, she grasped the cake bag and put it behind the desk. Julia breathed a sigh of relief.

"I take it you want to look at dresses?" Brooke marched around the desk, her hands clasped together. "You really should have started all of this much sooner, with your date being so close."

Dot, Sue, and Katie took it as their invitation to sit in the comfy crushed velvet chairs, and as though he could sense he was needed, Max appeared and poured them glasses of champagne. Brooke took Julia to one side and walked her through a series of rehearsed-sounding questions to figure out the style Julia wanted. She scribbled down the words 'simple, timeless, elegant' before searching the racks of white dresses. She assessed dozens, shaking her head and muttering to herself as she worked.

"This is all so exciting," Dot announced, draining her glass. She reached for the bottle and refilled it, ignoring Brooke and Max's side glances. "You're going to make the most beautiful bride."

"It's not like it's my first time doing this," Julia reminded them.

"Don't even go there," Sue jumped in. "This is so different than your first marriage. Jerad was an idiot, and you never should have married him, and we all said it. Barker is the real deal."

"I'll drink to that." Dot clinked her glass with Sue's. "He's certainly grown on me. It seems like he's always been there."

Julia knew exactly what Dot meant. It had only

been eighteen months since Barker had moved to Peridale as the plucky new detective inspector—and Julia's first impression of him hadn't been a good one. In fact, she vividly remembered how much she had disliked him. He had come across as an arrogant know-it-all, but something had changed along the way. His edges had softened, and Julia and Barker seemed to stick together like magnets. Julia hadn't been looking for love, but it had found her. They had been through so much since their first meeting, and she couldn't imagine her life without him.

Brooke cleared her throat, shaking Julia from her memories. She had three plastic-wrapped dresses draped over her arms for Julia to try on. While the trio continued drinking their champagne, Julia and Brooke headed into the large dressing room. Brooke left Julia to strip and wriggle into the first dress, joining her to lace the corset. Julia considered using their time alone to ask about her father, but the timing felt wrong. She wanted to be able to make a speedy exit if she needed to, and she couldn't imagine running out of the shop in a wedding dress.

"Follow me," Brooke instructed after whipping back the curtain.

They returned to the boutique, where a stool and

a three-way mirror had appeared in the middle of the shop. Dot, Sue, and Katie waited silently, perched on the edges of their seats, champagne temporarily forgotten. They shared a gasp when they saw her. Brooke helped Julia onto the stool in front of the mirror before stepping back to let her take in her reflection.

"Julia!" Dot sighed, producing a handkerchief from her bag. "I have no words!"

Julia hadn't expected to love the first dress she tried on, but she did. It had a sweetheart neckline, which flattered her décolletage and arms. The fabric on the bust trailed in a diagonal line down to her waist, somehow hiding her awkward bits and elongating her torso. The fabric hugged her hips in the right places before flaring out to the ground into a skirt with delicate lace detail. She turned to look at the back. It was open, but a semi-transparent lace panel covered her exposed skin.

"Princess Di *wishes* she had worn this dress," Dot exclaimed, dabbing at her eyes. "Just perfect!"

"I love it," Sue added. "It's you."

Julia's smile beamed back at her from the mirror. She was not wearing a hint of make-up, and her curly hair was pulled back into a high ponytail, and yet she felt more beautiful than she ever had in her whole life.

She glanced at Brooke in the mirror and found that though the woman's lips still formed in a tight line, the twinkle in her eyes revealed she was pleased with her selection.

"Your father is going to cry the minute he sees you," Katie said, dabbing at her eyes with her fingers. "Perfect."

Julia had gone to the bridal boutique to apologise, and more importantly, gather information. She had expected to try on a dress as part of the process, but she hadn't expected to fall head over heels in love.

"I never suggest buying the first dress you try on," Brooke stated, her voice its usual monotone hum, "but, I have to say, this dress was made for you. It will need taking up quite a bit, and I can already see a few alterations here and there." Brooke yanked on the waist to pull it in even more. "If you want it, we can definitely have this ready before the wedding. You're lucky I have Max here to perform the alterations. Most places outsource, which can slow things down. It's something to consider if you're planning to visit other shops."

"It's a real family-run business here," Julia said, emphasising the word 'family.'

"It's been in the family for three generations."

"Your mother?" Julia took her opportunity to dive

in.

"Yes," Brooke said quickly as she helped Julia off the step. "It used to be *Carol's Bridal Boutique*. I was in accounting, but my mother wanted to retire early to Oakwood Nursing Home, and I couldn't let this place go to a stranger. It's one of the few things I still have."

They retreated to the dressing room, and Brooke began to unlace the bodice. Julia let the silence linger for a moment, not wanting to appear too eager. She waited until Brooke was on the last set of laces before striking.

"Is your father at Oakwood with your mother?" Julia started, exhaling as the tight dress let go of her. "I think he was a drama teacher at my high school. Gary Williams?"

Brooke didn't respond, but Julia was sure the unlacing suddenly got more aggressive.

"You know who he is." Brooke's voice was flat and empty. "Don't play dumb. You said it yourself, you know what Leah did to our family. If you've come here to cause trouble, you can—"

"I just want to know what happened to him," Julia interrupted. "That's all."

There was another long pause while Brooke finished helping Julia out of the dress. She left the dressing room and yanked the curtain across to let Julia get back into her own clothes.

"He died," Brooke said bluntly through the curtain. "He killed himself, but as far as I'm concerned, Leah was the one who killed him. She took his career away from him, ruined his reputation, and he couldn't live with the aftermath. He might not have done anything to her, but accusations like that stick. They follow you around for the rest of your life, no matter how far away you try to run."

Back in her own clothes, Julia pulled back the curtain and handed Brooke the dress with a sympathetic smile. "I had no idea. I'm sorry."

"Me too," Brooke said, her jaw tightening. "He was my best friend." Brooke's bottom lip wobbled, but it stopped as quickly as it had started. "If you want this dress, it's £899, including two sets of alterations. I'd advise you not to decide yet. Would you like to try more?"

Julia considered the offer for a moment. The feeling the dress had given her could be addictive. A small, but very vocal, part of her brain screamed for her to try on as many as she could, but today was not the day. How could she do something so trivial when her best friend was still being questioned at the police station?

"Another time," Julia said. "It's getting late, and I don't want to keep you all night. I really do love that dress. You have great taste."

Brooke smiled her thanks before hanging the dress on a hook behind her. Brooked looped her hands together and fixed on Julia with an expectant look. The dry smile on her face sent a cold shiver across Julia's shoulders.

"Is there anything else you want to ask me?" Brooke's authoritarian tone reminded Julia of a school headmistress. "I saw you handing out those posters the other day. I asked around about you, and you have quite the reputation for playing detective."

"I've dabbled." Julia felt her cheeks redden. "I just want to find Leah and get to the bottom of things."

"Go on then."

"What?"

"Ask me where I was on the night of Leah's disappearance," Brooke demanded, her arms folding across her bony body. "You wouldn't be the first. The police barely waited for twenty-four hours before coming to see me. They looked at Leah's records and made the connection to my family in an instant. I'll tell you exactly what I told them—I was here all night with

Max. We had a delivery of the new season's dresses, and we stayed until the early hours of the morning to sort out the inventory. The delivery driver can confirm we were here at eight in the evening, and I gave the police the security camera footage to show we were both here all night. They haven't been in touch since, so if you want to ask that fiancé of yours to pull some strings at his old workplace, I'm sure you will, but I have nothing to hide." Brooke's chin darted up, her eyes narrowing. "Leah Burns has already done everything she could to ruin my family. She's not going to continue ruining it from wherever she is right now. If she's dead, it's what she deserves."

"Understood," was all Julia could say. "I'll go."

Brooke nodded, opening the door back into the boutique. Julia hurried through, nodding for Dot, Katie, and Sue to get moving. Dot downed her champagne before grabbing Sue's and finishing that too.

"I will hold this dress for one week," Brooke called after her. "It really was made for you."

Julia cast a smile over her shoulder, but she couldn't bring herself to look Brooke in the eye; she was sure the glare would turn her to stone. She hurried out of the shop, unable to remember the last time she had felt so exposed and embarrassed.

"There's still time to drop by another shop if you put your foot down." Sue checked her watch. "Although something tells me we didn't come here for dress shopping."

"Roxy was arrested last night," Julia revealed, glancing up the street at Roxy's pink front door. "Remember the hair I found? Roxy visited Leah before everything happened and she must have left behind another."

"Do you think she did it?" Dot asked, her eyes gleaming at the new gossip. "Poor Imogen! Two daughters and they both end up being murderers. What are the odds?"

"She didn't do it," Julia said firmly. "I know that for certain."

"How?" Sue asked, arching a brow. "Does that mean you know who did?"

"Not yet."

"So, how do you know?"

"Because she told me she didn't do it."

"And you believed her?" Dot let out a deep chuckle as she shook her head. "Oh, Julia! I never had you down as the naïve type. Of course, she wasn't going to tell you if she did it. The police certainly seem to think she's connected."

"Well, I don't." Julia pulled her keys from her pocket. "And I'm going to prove it."

"How?" Sue asked.

"I don't know yet, but I will."

# 11

J ulia pulled up outside The Plough after dropping everyone at their homes. She looked at the text message Barker had sent her while she was driving: 'Meet me at the pub. Turn right as soon as you walk in. You'll see me. URGENT!'

She dropped her phone into her bag and climbed out of the car. She stared at the police station across the road before checking her watch. DI Christie only had four more hours to charge Roxy before the twenty-four-hour hold window closed. For Roxy's sake, she hoped they didn't have anything other than a hair.

Walking past the outdoor tables full of people enjoying drinks in the early evening heat, Julia entered the pub. She followed Barker's instructions and immediately turned right. The pub was nearly empty, so it was not hard to spot Barker, even if all that could be seen of him were his darting eyes over the top of a menu. He motioned for her to hurry up and sit next to him. He opened a second menu and stuffed it in front of her face.

"Who are we hiding from?" Julia asked as she tried not to laugh at the silliness of the situation.

"Craig Wright." Barker jerked his head at the menu. "He's sat on the other side of the pub. I was working on my book. He came in as I was packing up. I don't think he's seen me yet. He's in a world of his own."

Julia attempted to peek over the menu, but Barker pulled it back up.

"Isn't this more obvious?" Julia laughed, the itch to look too strong to ignore. "Why can't we just go over and talk to him?"

"Because he looks like he's waiting for someone."

Barker's voice dropped to a whisper. "Don't you think it's a little suspicious that he's in the village considering everything that is happening? He said he hadn't been here in years, and now he's here waiting for someone?"

"That does sound a little suspicious," Julia replied, nodding her head, "but isn't this going to look even more suspicious? We *look* like we're trying to hide."

"We are."

"But do you want him to know that?" Julia dropped the menu and looked across the pub at Craig. "He's not even looking at us. He's staring off into space."

Barker carefully lowered his menu, keeping half his face covered. Julia tutted and snatched it off him and put it on the next table out of his reach. She glanced at Craig, who was a little more dressed up than he had been at his flat. He wore an ill-fitting black shirt with a white tie and creased, pinstriped pants. They were too short for him, showcasing his mismatching black and white socks and scuffed trainers.

"It looks like he got dressed in the dark," Barker remarked. "What's he doing here?"

It might not have been obvious to Barker, but it was to Julia. Craig was fiddling with a beer mat as his foot tapped on the floor. He checked his watch and fidgeted in his seat. After breathing into his hand and smelling the result, he slicked his palm over his shiny hair. Before Julia could reveal her theory, the door opened, and a woman entered. From the dark, ringlet curls cascading down her back, Julia was almost certain she knew who it was.

"I think that's Heidi," Julia whispered, picking up a menu and pretending to read it. "Johnny's half-sister."

"The jilted fiancé?"

"The very same." Julia peeked again. "She's not sitting down. Why do you think she's here?"

"To conspire?" Barker shrugged as he stole a glance. "She looks angry."

"Wouldn't you be angry if you came face-to-face with the man who left you at the altar for an eighteen-year-old? If we're to believe Craig, they haven't seen each other in years. That's a lot of festering."

"You don't sound like you believe that." Barker's searching gaze pierced her. "Do you think they're up to something?"

"It's a possibility."

"Well, they both hate Leah."

"Solid motives."

"Enough to want her out of the way after all these years?" Barker didn't sound sure. "Wouldn't they have moved on?"

"Does Craig seem like he's moved on to you?"

"Good point."

They looked away from each other at the same moment Heidi turned and stormed for the door. Julia had forgotten how much Heidi looked like her brother, right down to the pale skin, rosy cheeks, and glasses. Craig jumped up, looking like he was going to chase after her, but, instead, he sat back down and slammed the table with both fists.

"Wait here." Julia dropped the menu and stood. "I'm going to talk to her."

Julia darted out of the pub, catching the door before it closed. Heidi was already halfway up the street, her head low and her hands in her pockets.

"Heidi," Julia called after her as she jogged to catch up. "Heidi Watson?"

Heidi stopped and turned around. Tears flowed down her face. She squinted through them as she pulled off her glasses to wipe her eyes.

"*What*?" Heidi replied, a bitter edge to her voice. "Who are you?"

"My name is Julia. You probably don't remember me, but I'm a friend of your brother's."

"Right." Heidi nodded as she pushed her glasses back up her nose. "You're the girl who always made cakes."

"I'm less of a girl these days," Julia said with a light laugh, hoping to put Heidi at ease. "I just saw you in the pub. You seemed quite upset when you left. Are you okay?"

Heidi patted the tear streaks on her cheeks.

"I promised myself I wouldn't cry," Heidi said, stuffing her hands in her pockets as she took a step towards Julia. "I've cried enough tears over *him*."

"What happened?" Julia asked, deciding to let Heidi tell her story in her own words.

"He abandoned me on our wedding day." Heidi huffed, shaking her head up at the sky. "All these years later and it still hurts to say that. You think you get over these things, but it doesn't take much to drag you back. I was actually doing okay until I heard about Leah returning. I wish Johnny hadn't mentioned anything, but he called me right away. I think he thought he was doing me a favour, but just hearing her name knocked me sick." Heidi wiped away another tear as it rolled down her cheek. "And now she's missing, so, naturally, all the attention is once again on her. Craig contacted me on social media this afternoon. He said some random couple had gone to see him and asked him loads of questions about Leah. He said they asked about me, and it reminded him how much he missed me. *Ha!* Missed me? He makes it sounds like he didn't have a choice when he left me." She paused and inhaled. "He told me he'd be waiting for me at The Plough at six. I told myself I wasn't going to come. I try to stay away from this village as much as possible. Too many bad memories. I don't even know why I came. Maybe I thought I'd get some closure out of it? I should have realised it was far too late for that. Too much water under the bridge. I mean, he looks nothing like he did. He's majorly let himself go, and yet…"

"And yet?" Julia prompted.

"It sounds so idiotic." Heidi wiped away more tears. "It's been so many years. We were kids, but you never let go of the first boy who broke your heart, do you?" She grimaced. "I don't even know why I'm telling you this. I've bottled it up for so long. I'm sorry."

"You don't have to apologise," Julia said, offering a soft smile. "I own a café down the road if you want to get more off your chest? It's quiet and private, and I have some leftover brownies."

Heidi considered the invitation before shaking her head. "Thanks, but I should go. I just want to go home and pretend this didn't happen."

"Why don't you drop by Johnny's?" Julia

suggested. "You shouldn't be on your own when you're like this."

"We're not on the best speaking terms right now. He turned up on my doorstep acting weird earlier this week after months of not speaking to me. He said he'd done something stupid, but he wouldn't tell me what. I wasn't in the mood for games, so I let him sleep on the couch, and I went to bed. He was gone by the morning."

"Do you remember what day that was?"

"Tuesday," Heidi said without thinking about it. "Is it important?"

"No." Julia smiled as she shook her head. "I was just curious. Well, it was nice seeing you, Heidi. Try not to let Craig get you down too much."

Heidi nodded, her eyes narrowing on Julia.

"I never told you his name," Heidi said, her arms crossing together. "Do you know him?"

Julia's mind blasted into overdrive as she tried to think of something to say. She felt like an idiot for slipping up when Heidi was about to leave. She had been so cool and collected gathering her information and busting Johnny's alibi wide open. When Julia's phone started ringing in her bag, she didn't bother holding in the sigh of relief.

"I need to get this," Julia said when she saw Jessie's face on the screen. "Sorry."

Julia answered the call and put it to her ear. The temporary relief she had felt was quickly replaced with panic when she realised it must have been the early hours in the morning in Australia.

"Jessie?" Julia called into her phone. "Is everything okay?"

"*Mum?*" Jessie bellowed over pounding music. "You there?"

"Yes, I'm here." She smiled her apologies to Heidi before turning around. "Go somewhere I can hear you."

Julia listened to what sounded like Jessie pushing through a crowd of people, mumblings of 'move!' and 'get out of my way!' blasting through the speaker. A door slammed, and the music was reduced to a distant thumping.

"What's up?" Jessie said, her voice echoing. "I'm in a nightclub."

"You sound drunk."

"I am."

"*Jessie!*"

"I'm eighteen," Jessie replied with a chuckle. "What do you want?"

"You called me."

"Oh, right." Jessie paused and hummed for over half a minute. "What was I supposed to say?"

"Is something wrong? Put Alfie on the phone."

"I'm in the girl's bathroom. I remember now. I've lost my bank card, and I need you to go home and find one of my statements, so I can call the bank and cancel."

"You've lost your card?"

"*Don't worry!*" Jessie cried. "Listen, just take a picture of one and text it to me, okay? I'm going to get back. I'm having so much fun. Love you!"

Jessie hung up before Julia could respond. Turning around, she saw Heidi had already left. Glad she hadn't needed to explain her slip up, Julia returned to the pub. Craig was drowning his sorrows in a pint, and Barker was back behind his menu.

"Jessie's lost her bank card," Julia explained. "I'm going to head home. She needs a statement. Are you coming?"

"I'm going to stay here for a while." Barker glanced over his menu. "I want to see what he does next."

Leaving Barker to his stake-out, Julia drove up the winding lane to her cottage. The forensic team had abandoned Leah's house, leaving behind a wrapping of blue and white police tape. Julia had considered having a look around, but she doubted much could be left to find.

Julia considered what Heidi had revealed about Johnny. Heidi had unknowingly destroyed her half-brother's alibi, while simultaneously putting him back in the frame. She retrieved her phone as she walked down the garden path to the front door. When she attempted to call Johnny, it went straight to the voicemail. She waited until the phone beeped for her to leave her message.

"Johnny, it's Julia. I need to talk to you. I know you lied about your alibi. Call me back as soon as you get this."

Julia hung up and dropped the phone back into her bag, trading it for her keys. As she reached out to unlock her door, two sets of hands gripped her arms, yanking them back. Before she could turn around to see who was there, a dark hood dropped over her head.

# 12

J ulia thrashed and kicked as her two mystery assailants dragged her down the garden path. She screamed out, one thing on her mind—she couldn't end up like Leah.

Her elbow struck something hard, and one pair of hands let go. A female voice cried out. The second set seemed less sure of their grip without assistance. Sensing her opportunity, Julia grabbed at her attacker, finding the arms slender and bony under her touch. Using her body weight, she spun around, sending her attacker in the same direction as the person she had elbowed. The second assailant let go with little resistance, yelping as they fell to the ground.

Julia stumbled back, feet going from the path to the grass. The shallow dip between the two shifted her centre of gravity, pulling her to the ground with a thud. She imagined the attackers readying for their second attempt and knew she couldn't let them get hold of her. She ripped the hood off, only to find her vision blocked by her messy hair. Frenzied cries escaped her lips as she fought with the curls blocking her vision.

"*Julia!*" a familiar, muffled voice called out. "It's *us*! Calm down!"

Julia parted her hair and looked up at Sue, who was holding her bloody nose with one hand and offering the other to Julia. Confused, Julia reached out and stood up, gasping for air. Dot lay on the other side of the path, clutching her side.

"It's fine!" Dot cried, waving her hand as she pushed herself up. "Don't help the octogenarian up!"

"I don't understand," Julia muttered, her face hot as her heart thrashed in her chest. "What on earth were you trying to do?"

"Kidnap you," Sue offered with a pathetic smile, a trickle of blood escaping her pinching fingers. "We should have known you'd put up a fight."

Dot dusted the dry grass off her skirt and limped over to the path. She reached into her handbag and passed Sue a handkerchief for her nose.

"Why would you want to kidnap me?" Julia cried, stepping back. "Is there something you want to tell me?"

Dot and Sue glanced at each other, their expressions equally offended.

"She thinks we bumped Leah off." Dot shook her head as she laughed. "Good heavens, dear! I suppose it does look like that, doesn't it? I don't think we thought this plan out."

"*Your* plan," Sue mumbled through the hankie. "We wanted to do something nice for you, so you could unwind for one night."

"And you thought grabbing me and putting a bag over my head would help me *unwind*?" Julia kicked the hood onto the path. "Have you lost your minds?"

"Well, when you put it like that, it does sound rather problematic." Dot adjusted her brooch as her neck stiffened. "Oh, we might as well give it up. Sue, give the signal."

Sue pulled her phone out of her back, turned on the flash, and waved it above her head. Seconds later, a familiar pink Range Rover sped down the lane, stopping inches behind Julia's car. The blacked-out window zipped down, and Katie stuck her head out.

"Oh, no fun!" Katie squeaked. "I thought we were waiting until we were back at my house to unmask her?"

Julia planted her hands on her hips and glowered at them for an explanation.

"We were going to take you to Peridale Manor for a surprise party," Dot said with a sigh. "An early hen party, of sorts. Not your official one, of course, but enough to give you a night off from your Leah hunting."

"I even brought these." Katie hung a handful of pink feather boas out of the window. "I bought a case of classy champagne, and Hilary's put some food together for us."

"We were going to listen to music and play silly games." Sue pulled the bloody hankie away from her nose and gave her nostrils a wriggle. "Perhaps we started the games a little too early."

"Perhaps," Julia replied flatly. "Didn't you think it was a bit on the nose, considering what happened across the road?" She nodded at Leah's cottage. "A little too soon for kidnapping games, some might say?"

"Lighten up, dear." Dot waved her hand and

walked towards the Range Rover. She grabbed a boa from Katie and wrapped it around her neck. "Well, are you coming, or not? Because I'm not missing out on expensive champagne and good posh food."

"Sorry, Julia," Sue offered, her voice stuffy. "I feel like a bit of an idiot right now. I should have seen how this could turn out. I should have known you would turn Rambo on us."

"It's fine." Julia tucked her hair behind her ears and tried to calm herself as the adrenaline coursed through her veins. "Sorry about your nose."

"Collateral damage."

Julia followed Sue to the pink SUV, grabbing a boa from Katie before climbing inside. As they sped through the village towards the manor, Julia forced herself to calm down. It was such a ridiculous idea, only Dot could have come up with it. The sentiment touched Julia, even if the execution of their mock-kidnap had shaken her badly.

Peridale Manor was the biggest home in the village. It had belonged to the Wellington family for generations, and it currently belonged to Katie's elderly, wheelchair-bound father, Vincent Wellington. It sat on acres of beautiful countryside, and a sprawling driveway led up to the grand building. The house still took Julia's breath away every time she drove up to it.

In the couple of hours since Julia had dropped them all off, they had been busy. Bright pink balloons covered the grand entrance and stairway, and bubbly pop music drifted in from the sitting room. Hilary, the housekeeper, had arranged a spread more suited for a party of twenty on the marble kitchen island, and the promised champagne stood on the side, four bottles already chilling in their dedicated silver ice buckets.

"I wish Jessie was here," Julia found herself saying as she looked at all the effort that had been put in. "She'd probably hate all this, but I can't imagine my hen party without her."

"We'll have another one," Sue said as she ran a cloth under the tap to dab at her nose. "This is the unofficial pre-hen hen party."

"Besides, Jessie knows what we're doing," Dot said as she hurried past Julia into the kitchen. "How do you think we got you up to your cottage at the right time?"

"So, she didn't lose her bank card?"

"That was my idea!" Katie proclaimed proudly. "I did the same thing when I was in Ibiza at her age."

"She sounded like she was having a whale of a time," Dot mumbled through a mouthful of a sandwich. "I hated to drag her away from her party, but she was up for playing a little trick on you."

"Is that how the history books are going to remember it? A little trick?"

"A *big* trick, then." Dot rolled her eyes. "Fill up a plate and let's get this party started! And no mention of anything connected to *you-know-who*!"

Julia did as she was told. When all their plates were heaped with food, they retreated into the lavish sitting room, decorated with pink balloons attached to anything that would take a string. They sat in couples on the ornate sofas in the middle of the room, and it didn't take long for Julia to forget about her earlier ordeal. The champagne and music washed over her, making her feel the most relaxed she had since Jessie left for Australia.

"Okay, question time!" Katie announced, pulling a stack of pink cards from a box. "Are you ready to be tested on your relationship with Barker?"

"Ready as I'll ever be." Julia drained her second refill of champagne.

"When did you first meet Barker?"

"That's easy!" Dot cried as she topped up their glasses with a fresh bottle. "Even I could tell you that one."

"It's the question on the card!" Katie pouted

before turning and smiling at Julia. "Besides, I don't think I've ever heard it."

It was an easy story for Julia to recount. It felt like yesterday and a lifetime ago at the same time.

"Barker was moving to the village," she started, a fond smile washing over her face. "His moving van was blocking the lane into the village. I pulled up behind him and asked him to move so I could get past. I think I tried to start a conversation about the weather, but he didn't take me on. Oh, I thought he was so arrogant! He kept calling me 'Julie', and I think he only did it because he knew it irritated me. I remember thinking that nothing about him fit this village."

"What a romantic story," Dot said sarcastically. "And you still fell in love with him?"

"I think it's sweet!" Katie clasped her hands together. "They obviously had chemistry from the moment they met. If he wanted to get under her skin, it means he liked her from the start." Katie flipped to the next question. "What was your first official date?"

"Dinner at The Comfy Corner," Julia answered quickly. "It was about a month after he actually asked me on a date, but I thought he had got cold feet. I think he was just nervous."

"That's a good sign," Katie butted in. "Your father

was like that when he asked me out for the first time. Turned him into a bumbling schoolboy. What did you eat?"

"We both had the Peridale Pie. Mary put us in the restaurant's lover's corner, and it couldn't have been more obvious that she was spying on us the whole time."

"So romantic." Katie sighed as she gazed into the corner of the room. "I love Peridale Pie."

"Oh, give me those!" Dot snatched the cards from Katie. "These are all so dreary. We've heard these stories a billion times. Let me see what's in here." She flicked through, throwing them over her shoulder one by one. "Oh, this is a good one!"

"You can't ask *that*!" Katie snatched the cards back, her cheeks blushing. "It's too rude." She shuffled through the cards before settling on one. "What's your favourite thing about Barker?"

"He makes me feel safe," Julia replied. "I feel comfortable around him. It never feels like either of us is ever trying to be anything other than ourselves. We click."

"Like pieces of a jigsaw." Sue chinked her glass against Julia's. "Just like Neil and me."

"And your father and me." Katie leaned in and hit

her glass against theirs.

"And me and me." Dot joined in. "I don't want to feel left out."

"There's lots of things you click with," Sue said. "Like gossip, and trouble-starting, and offending."

"You think I'm a gossip?"

"Is the Pope Catholic?"

Laughter erupted, echoing around the room. Even Dot joined in, rolling back in her chair before draining her glass. She hiccoughed, causing more laughter, and more hiccoughs. Julia felt so grateful to have these women in her life, but someone other than Jessie missing; Roxy should have been there. Her laughter faltered long enough for the gloom to creep in. She sipped her champagne hoping to retreat into its fizzy warmth, but the bubble had burst.

"What's wrong?" Sue asked, noticing Julia's change in an instant. "Julia?"

"It doesn't matter." She pushed forward a smile. "More questions, Katie."

Katie shuffled the cards, but she looked unsure about continuing. Dot took them off her and threw them onto the table. Leaning forward, Dot rested her elbows on the hem of her skirt and reached across to grab Julia's hands.

"Is it Leah?"

"Sort of," Julia replied, clutching her gran's hands. "Right now, it's more Roxy. I shouldn't be drinking champagne and laughing while she's still at the station being questioned. They're probably putting her through hell."

"You didn't make her go to Leah's cottage," Dot said forcefully, shaking Julia's hands. "She's a grown woman. If she killed Leah—"

"Gran," Sue interrupted, shaking her head. "Let's not go there."

"Someone needs to say it, dear." Dot sighed, dropping her head. "It's been five days, and there's been neither sight nor sound of her. You know she's probably dead."

"I know," Julia replied, the words jamming in her throat. "I've known since the second I saw that blood."

Julia was not just saying the words out loud for the first time; she was admitting them to herself, too. Saying them felt freeing and heart-breaking at the same time. Through all the shocking revelations and accusations connected to Leah's past, she had clung to a tiny glimmer of hope that she would get an explanation from the source. Now, she felt her spirit let that hope go. She deflated into the sofa, drained and exhausted from the chaos her life had been in the week since Leah's return to the village.

"Let it out," Dot urged. "Scream and cry. Smash this place up if you need to. Katie doesn't mind, do you, Katie?"

"Well, I—"

"Exactly," Dot cut in. "Nobody will judge you for letting go, Julia. We love you, but it's okay to admit defeat. You've done enough. Let it go. You don't need to solve and fix everything every time."

It was a tempting offer. Accepting that this was one mystery she couldn't solve would be the easy way out. The police might eventually untangle the case, and if they couldn't, did it really matter? Julia considered that question for a moment, but the answer was obvious.

"It's not just for me," she said after exhaling. "My friends are involved. Johnny and Roxy put themselves in the middle of this, and I need to help them. Not for my satisfaction, but because I don't want to see them dragged down with the ship. The police are scrambling for anything right now, and if someone doesn't figure this out, an innocent person's life might be ruined."

"And it might not."

"It's not a risk I'm willing to take."

Julia tugged her hands from Dot's and pulled her

phone from her pocket. The words on her screen were blurry thanks to the champagne. She wanted to call Johnny again, but there was a text message that had been sent six minutes ago.

"It's Barker," she explained. "He wants to know where I am."

She replied, telling him she was at the manor. He read the message instantly, and three bubbles appeared to show that he was typing. 'On my way' popped up within seconds.

"He's coming up." Julia tapped her phone against her chin. "It must be important." She looked around at the balloons and the barely-touched food on their plates. "I'm sorry. I feel like I've wasted your time."

"Did it take your mind off things for an hour?" Dot asked.

"Yes."

"Then it was worth it." Dot twinkled with a lively smile. "You take on so much, it was nice to take you out of it, if only for a little while."

"Maybe think about not trying to abduct me next time?"

"I'll consider it."

They nibbled their food and finished their drinks while they waited for Barker. When the doorbell rang, they all jumped up and hurried into the hallway. Hilary, the housekeeper, appeared at the top of the stairs with her cane, waving her free hand and heading back to her room when she saw them running for the door. Julia ripped open the door as the bell sounded again. She let out a shriek when she saw that it was Roxy and not Barker who was standing on the doorstep. Julia dove forward, grabbing her friend into the tightest hug she had ever given her.

"They had nothing on me," Roxy said as she clung to Julia. "They've been drilling me to confess every second since they took me in."

"I'm so glad to see you."

"I'm sorry, Julia." Roxy dug her face into her shoulder. "You've been through too much. I promise I didn't kill Leah. I swear on Violet's life I didn't even touch her."

"I believe you."

"We all do," Dot said, followed by a cough. "Well, now that they haven't charged you with anything."

Julia opened her eyes and looked over Roxy's shoulder. Barker stood beside his car. From the way he was wringing his hands, she knew there was more. She reluctantly let go of Roxy and crossed over to him.

"There's been a development," he said, his tone

careful and low.

"A development?"

"They've found a body." He swallowed hard before exhaling. "They want you to go and identify it."

Agatha Frost

# 13

Barker eased in between two cars at the far side of the busy car park before reaching out and resting a hand on Julia's knee.

"You don't have to do this."

"Don't I?"

"Christie will just have to wait for the official identification process."

"I want to."

"Are you sure?"

"I *need* to."

Julia looked at the hospital as the setting sun turned the surrounding sky dusky pink. She imagined Leah in there, lifeless and lying on a table. Or would she be in a body bag? The thought turned Julia's stomach. It had already been a bizarre day, and it was about to get even stranger. She pinched her wrist, but she was very much awake.

"What will she look like?" Julia asked.

"I don't know." Barker gulped. "Christie said they'd only just found her. She'll be in the state she was when they brought her in. This isn't usually how things are done. We—I mean *they*—normally let the pathologist do their job, clean the body up a bit, and let the family identify the person from a photograph. You honestly don't have to do this."

"I do." Julia opened the door and climbed out. "Let's just get this over with."

They wove between the parked cars and walked towards the hospital hand in hand. Instead of going to the entrance, Barker took her around the side, and they followed the wall until they reached a metal fire door. He banged on it with his fist. It opened immediately. DI Christie poked his head out before ushering them in. Thick stubble covered the lower half of his face, his eyes were red and hollow, and his suit looked like it had been evading the washing machine. Had he slept since the beginning of the case?

"Nobody saw you, did they?" he asked after sucking on an electronic cigarette. "I could lose my job over this."

He blew a fruity cloud of chalky smoke in their direction before taking another long drag.

"Raspberry?" Julia asked.

"Is there anything you don't know?"

"Baker's nose."

Christie's mouth hardened into a straight line. "Wife is making me give up. It's like sucking on fresh air, and these don't help either." He yanked up his sleeve to show three nicotine patches on his forearm. "I would kill for a real cigarette right about now. I've never felt more stressed in my life. How did you do it, Barker?"

"One day at a time."

"At this rate, I don't think I'll be here for another day." He glanced at a set of double doors. "She's in there. One of the patrol cars found her at the side of the road an hour ago. She looks like the few pictures of Leah we have, but I need to be sure."

"How did she die?" Julia asked, her mouth drying.

"I don't know." Christie took one last drag on his device before pocketing it. "I've only seen her face, so all I know is that she wasn't shot in the head." He offered an awkward laugh but immediately cut it short when they didn't join in. "Pathologist hasn't arrived to perform the post-mortem yet. He'll be here any minute, so we need to be quick. You can't linger too long. Are you ready?"

Julia stared at the double doors and tried to swallow, but she had no moisture left in her mouth. She attempted to nod, but her head barely moved. She was sure no one could ever feel 'ready' for such an occasion.

Christie took her head jerk as confirmation. He pulled one of the double doors open a fraction and waved them through it. They entered a dimly lit, freezing examination room. Stainless steel counters topped with trays of gleaming tools lined the room. A large window occupied one of the walls, offering a view of a second, darker room. The current room's light illuminated the vaguest outline of a body on a table.

"You really don't have to do this," Barker whispered, grabbing her hand. "These things never leave you."

But before Julia could change her mind, Christie flicked a switch on the wall. Strips of lights illuminated one by one, revealing the body from the feet up. A blue sheet covered most of it, but the sheet had been folded down at the neck to leave the face uncovered. If the body hadn't been so motionless, she could have been sleeping. Her face had cuts and bruises, and her pale hair was matted and full of twigs and leaves. It was the saddest sight Julia had ever seen. She bit back the tears as she turned away.

"That's not her," she croaked. "That's not Leah."

"*What*?" Christie cried. "It *has* to be."

"It's not." Julia closed her eyes, but she could still see the woman. "I've known Leah since childhood. That's not her."

"I don't understand." Christie's hands disappeared into his thinning hair as he stared at the woman on the table. "Maybe you're wrong? Take another look."

Julia reluctantly took a second glance at the woman. She could see why Christie thought they were the same person. They looked to be similar ages and builds, and their hair was even a similar shade of sandy blonde, but the differences were obvious to Julia. The stranger had sunken cheekbones, a hooked thin nose, and a jutting chin.

"I'm sure."

"It can't be!"

"She said she's sure." Barker pulled Julia into his shirt. "Back off, Christie. I know what it's like to want something to be true, but if Julia says it's not her, it's not."

Christie glared at them both, and then at the woman in the other room. He cried out and crashed both fists onto the counter. The tools jumped and rattled. A moment later, Christie turned away and pushed violently through the doors. They swung in his wake, admitting the hot air from the corridor.

Julia stole one last glance at the woman. She sympathised with whatever she had been through, but she was glad she was not Leah. She turned away and leaned into Barker before they walked through the still swinging doors. Christie leaned against the wall, his electronic cigarette clasped between his tight lips. He sucked and exhaled in one motion, breathing plumes of smoke like a furious dragon.

"I thought this was my breakthrough." He kicked the wall with the heel of his shoe. "Chief has been breathing down my neck since day one to come up with something, but it's like the woman vanished into thin air. I thought she'd just fallen into my lap, but now I have a Jane Doe on my hands, which is the last thing I need."

"Do you have no leads?" Barker asked.

"*Nothing!*" Christie cried. "Forensics raked over her house with a fine-toothed comb, and all they came up with were fingerprints on the side table and some unknown male DNA in the bedsheets. We matched the prints to Roxy, but the male DNA doesn't match anyone in our system. Do you have any ideas?"

Julia shook her head, even though she remembered what Roxy had said about hearing someone snoring upstairs during her visit.

"I couldn't get anything from Roxy," he continued. "I tried to press her for a confession, but she wouldn't give me anything. Her timeline of leaving Leah's, going to the shop, and then the school checks out with security footage we gathered from around the village. A fingerprint wasn't enough to charge her, so I had to release her. It's an embarrassment! My first big case as DI and every lead I've followed has fizzled into nothing." He turned to Julia as he ran his hands against his stubble. "Please tell me you have something. I know you've been flitting around the village."

Julia immediately thought about what Heidi had told her about Johnny, but there was no way she was going to reveal that to Christie without first speaking to her friend.

"Have you looked into Leah's first ex-husband?" Julia asked the second it came to her mind. "Craig Wright. He lives over at Fern Moore. Flat 104. I saw him in the village today."

"Craig Wright?" Christie pulled a pad and pen from his pocket. "His name hasn't come up. Do you think he's connected?"

"I don't know," Julia admitted. "But he left the village with Leah, and they had a messy divorce. We went to see him, and his alibi is shaky. It might be worth talking to him."

"Got it." Christie scribbled on his pad. "Anything else?"

"No," Julia replied. "That's all I've got."

Christie looked up at her, and she knew he didn't believe it, but she remained calm. Until she spoke to Johnny, she was not handing him over to the police.

"You should go." Christie walked them over to the door and opened it. "Not a word of this to anyone, got it?"

"We won't say anything," Barker said. "Are you going to be okay? You need to take care of yourself, or you're going to burn out."

"I'll be fine." Christie waved his hand before reaching for his electronic cigarette again. "I'm going to wait for the pathologist to see what happened to my Jane Doe."

"Promise you'll take care of yourself?" Barker slapped him on the shoulder. "It can be a tough job."

"Okay, I promise," he muttered between drags on his device. "Thanks for coming."

They walked into the dark, Barker shutting the door behind them. They lingered for a moment before holding hands and setting off.

"There is more, isn't there?" Barker asked when the car park came into view. "It was written all over your face that you were holding something back."

"I need to work on my poker face."

"It was quite good, but I know you." Barker smiled. "Has something new happened?"

"You know how Johnny's alibi was that he was at his cottage with Heidi all night?"

"You didn't believe him."

"And I was right not to." Julia looked around to make sure they were alone. "Heidi said she hadn't seen Johnny in months until he turned up on her doorstep crying that he'd done something wrong. Guess what night that was?"

"Tuesday?"

"Bingo."

"Do you think he killed Leah?"

"I'm not jumping to that conclusion until I speak to him." Julia sighed and rubbed her head. "But even I have to admit it doesn't look good."

"But it's Johnny." Barker laughed and shook his head. "He wouldn't hurt a fly. I don't think he could if he wanted to."

Usually, Julia would have agreed with Barker, but she remembered Johnny's near-rabid reaction when she had sprung Leah on him in the café. It had been a side of Johnny she had never seen, and it had scared her.

"I need to find him." Julia checked her watch. "Why don't you stay here and make sure Christie is alright? Maybe take him to the canteen to get something to eat. The poor man looks like he's on the brink."

"Do you mind?" Barker asked, sucking the air through his teeth as though he had wanted to ask. "I really feel for the guy. It's a tough job."

"I'll grab a taxi back to the village. I'll let you know if I find Johnny. I thought everything that could have happened today had already happened, but it turns out the day isn't done with me yet."

"What else has occurred?"

"Wedding dress shopping, kidnapping." Julia tried

to laugh, but she was too exhausted to make a joke of it. "It's just been a long day. Although, speaking of wedding dress shopping, something interesting happened while I was there."

"Did you find a dress?"

"Sort of, but that's not it. Brooke told me the police had already been to see her and she gave them security video footage of her at the shop at the time Leah disappeared. It's probably nothing, but do you think you could get the footage to review it?"

"Consider it done." Barker nodded. "Christie owes us after what we just did. I shouldn't be here for too long. Let me know if you find Johnny."

"I will."

"And stay safe."

She smiled. "Of course."

# 14

The taxi driver remained silent for the journey back to Peridale, giving Julia a chance to formulate a plan. She was going to have a quick shower, drink a very strong coffee, and go in search of Johnny, not stopping until she found him. When the taxi pulled up to her cottage, it seemed the plan wasn't necessary at all.

"Keep the change," she told the driver as she climbed out of the cab.

Johnny sat on Julia's doorstep next to a large suitcase. His head was in his hands, and he seemed so deep in thought that he hadn't heard the taxi. Julia cleared her throat as she unclipped her gate. His head darted up.

"Going on holiday?" she asked as she nodded at the case. "Or are you trying to move in?"

"Heidi called me," he said quietly. "She told me what you asked her."

"If you were going to involve her in your lie, maybe you should have told her first?" Julia smiled as she joined him on the doorstep. "What's with the case?"

"I panicked and packed a bag. I went to the train station and convinced myself I was going to get on the first train that pulled into the station. I missed the first one, and the second. I tried to tell myself that I was waiting for a destination I liked the sound of, but I knew I didn't want to run away. I love Peridale. Why should I have to leave? I haven't done anything wrong. Not really. I didn't *kill* Leah."

"Why don't we go inside and talk about this over a cup of tea?" Julia helped him up off the step. "You look like you need one."

Johnny nodded and looked pathetically at the ground. Julia rummaged for her keys and unlocked the door. Grabbing the suitcase, Julia dragged it into the hallway before leading Johnny into the sitting room. She planted him in an armchair.

"Stay there," she ordered.

She hurried into the kitchen and filled the kettle. Mowgli sauntered in from the bedroom. He yawned as he stretched out each leg in turn. He shook out his fur right down to the end of his tail before jumping onto the counter. He gave her his 'where have you been?' meow as he headbutted her.

"It's been a long day, boy," she whispered to him, tickling his head. "I'll tell you all about it later."

She filled his food bowl before grabbing two cups from the cupboard. She put a black tea bag in one and a peppermint and liquorice in the other. She filled them to the brim when the kettle pinged, and after letting them steep for a couple of minutes, she added milk and plenty of sugar to the black tea; Johnny looked like he needed it.

In the sitting room, Johnny stood at the mantlepiece in the dark, a photograph in his hand. From the frame, Julia knew it was a picture of her with Barker and Jessie at the top of Blackpool Tower, taken on a recent holiday.

"You have it all," Johnny said as he put the picture

back. "You really landed on your feet with those two. I'm happy for you."

"But I detect a hint of jealousy in your voice."

"I *am* jealous."

"Oh, Johnny. It's not too late for you. We're still young!"

"Are we?" Johnny sighed. "I don't feel it. I'm heading into my forties, and I've never had a relationship that's lasted more than a couple of months. You're about to get married for the second time."

"And look how my first marriage ended." Julia passed him his cup and nodded for him to sit down. She switched on a table lamp and sat on the edge of the couch. "I married a pig, lived unhappily with him for twelve years, and then crawled back to Peridale to restart my entire life from scratch. Do you know how hard that is to do in your thirties?"

"But you did it."

"And *you'll* find someone." Julia tapped him on the knee. "The right woman is out there for you. You'll find her when you least expect it."

Johnny scoffed before blowing on the surface of his tea. Julia felt for him. He had always been unlucky in love—surprising because he was one of the nicest men she knew. When they were teenagers, he had once confessed his love to her, but she had never looked at him like that. She'd felt guilty about it for years, and had even gone on a date with him when she returned to the village after her marriage ended, but they didn't have that kind of chemistry. She had hoped he had let go of her, but the look in his eyes as he stared at her over the surface of his tea told her something different.

"What happened on Tuesday night, Johnny?" Julia asked him. "And I want the truth this time. No more lies. Heidi said you turned up at her house in a state. Is that true?"

He nodded.

"So, what happened?"

"I didn't want to lie to you," he started. "I almost told you the truth when you confronted me about the article I posted through your door, but the timing didn't feel right. I knew how it would look. I didn't want you to jump to conclusions."

"About what?"

"About what happened with Leah." He paused and sipped his hot tea. "I went to see her on Tuesday night, and something happened."

"What did you do?"

"I didn't kill her."

"You've said that."

"But you have got to believe me." His voice rose. "I didn't kill her."

"I'm not saying you did, but what did you do?"

"Something stupid." He looked up at the ceiling as he exhaled. "Do you remember Roxy's seventeenth birthday party?"

Julia nodded. She almost told him it was not the first time someone had asked her that question recently, but she stopped herself when she realised Johnny didn't know about what had happened between Roxy and Leah.

"That was the first time I'd ever tried alcohol," he continued. "Everyone else was drinking, so I joined in. We'd just left school, and it felt like the perfect time to reinvent myself. I'd lost some weight, and my skin had cleared up during the summer. I wanted to be cool."

"You were always cool to me, Johnny."

"Well, I wasn't to the rest of them." He laughed. "I was terminally uncool, so I drank. I didn't like the taste of it in the slightest, but I liked how it made me feel. All my worries floated away, and I *felt* cool. It was as fun as everyone had said it was. People told me I was funny for the first time in my life, so I drank some more. I had the tolerance of a small bird, so I was drunk in no time." He paused and sipped more of his tea. "About halfway through the night, I went to the bathroom. I should have knocked, but being drunk removed my manners. Leah was in there reapplying her lipstick in the mirror. It was bright red and smeared all over her chin. I didn't realise it at the time, but she'd probably been kissing someone."

Julia knew exactly who Leah had kissed, but this was not the time to reveal that information; she could already sense what was coming next.

"I lost my virginity to Leah that night." Johnny stared down into his tea as his cheeks flushed with colour. "I'm not proud of it. I didn't plan it, it just happened. One minute I was apologising, and the next minute we were all over each other. It was just like that instant chemistry that you see in the films. I couldn't believe it was happening until it was over. I woke up the next morning in Roxy's bath with a banging headache. I nearly forgot what happened, but I had lipstick all over my face. I was so embarrassed and ashamed of myself. I found Leah downstairs making tea in the kitchen. She didn't even seem slightly phased by what had happened. When I asked her if we could talk about it, she just shrugged and said it wasn't important."

"Oh, Johnny."

"I felt like a mug!" he cried. "I'd thrown *it* away. I

215

thought we were friends, but she treated me like a stranger. I tried to talk to her on more than one occasion, but she never answered the phone, so I gave up. It was a kick in the guts when she ran off with Craig. I never saw her again until—"

"Until I paraded her in front of you at my café," Julia interrupted. "I'm so sorry."

"You weren't to know. I've never told a soul until today." He sipped more tea. "All these emotions stirred up in me when I saw her. I was angry because of what she did to my sister, angry at what she did to me, shocked that she had the nerve to come back and act like nothing had happened. I went to see her to get an explanation."

"What happened?"

"I got to her cottage full of all that anger, and I expected her to brush me off, but she apologised. She apologised about what happened between us, and what she did to my sister. She sounded like she meant it. I didn't know what to do. We talked, and she explained that a lot had happened since then. She'd grown up and seemed remorseful about the things she did back then. I was about to leave, but I made another terrible mistake."

"Just tell me, Johnny!"

"The same mistake I made when I was seventeen," he groaned. "I looked into her eyes for too long, and that spark happened again. All these years later, and I was suddenly in that bathroom at Roxy's party. It just exploded. We went upstairs to her bedroom, and we— please, don't make me say it."

"I can fill in the blanks."

"I went there to confront her, and I ended up in her bed." He paused and inhaled deeply. "I fell asleep, and I didn't wake up until I heard a bang. She wasn't next to me. I got dressed and went downstairs, but she wasn't there. I saw a lamp and broken ornaments on the floor. I was so confused. I didn't know what to do. I promise I didn't see the blood, or I would have called the police. I ran, and I didn't stop running until I was at Heidi's cottage. I don't know why I went there. I think I thought she was the only person who would understand, but how could I tell her that I'd just slept with the woman who ruined her life all those years ago? I know how it looks, and you don't have to believe me, but I didn't hurt a hair on her head."

"I believe you."

"You do?"

"I don't think you have any reason to lie to me at this point." Julia rested her hand on his. "I thought you were trying to protect Heidi, but you were just trying to protect yourself."

"You thought Heidi had something to do with it?"

"I considered her, but if she was at her cottage when you arrived, her involvement is virtually impossible." Julia sipped her tea. "It doesn't bring me any closer to figuring this out though. The only person who doesn't have an alibi right now is Craig, and he seemed surprised when I told him about Leah. Maybe he's a good actor."

"*Craig?*" Johnny laughed. "From what I remember, he wasn't the sharpest tool in the box. I don't think he'd be able to lie about something so big. What about Gary Williams? I thought I had it all figured out when I sent you that article. I wasn't trying to mess with you. I genuinely thought it would point you in the right direction. You didn't need to know what I did to figure it out."

"Gary's dead."

"Oh."

"Suicide."

"Poor guy." Johnny pinched between his brows. "I probably should have looked that up before passing it onto you, being a journalist and all. This is what I don't understand about Leah. Why did she ruin so many lives? It doesn't make any sense. Was she a sociopath?"

"I wish I knew, Johnny. I really do."

"And we might never get an explanation. Do you think there's any chance she's still alive?"

"I did," Julia admitted. "And then I didn't, and then I *really* didn't when I was asked to view a body that the police were convinced was her. But, it wasn't, and now I honestly don't know. I hope she is."

"Me too." Johnny blushed. "I don't want to leave it how we did. No matter what else she did, she was our friend once upon a time. Do you really have nothing else to work with?"

Julia stood and motioned for Johnny to follow her into the dining room. She flicked on the light to reveal the investigation wall Barker had put together the night before. Pieces of paper with all the information they knew filtered down from a copy of Leah's missing poster. Julia tugged 'Johnny', 'Heidi', and 'Roxy' off the list of suspects, leaving behind 'Craig' and 'Brooke.'

"If Gary weren't dead, I'd have said he had the best motive to want Leah out of the way. Did you say Brooke had an alibi?"

"She said she was at her shop with her son all night. Apparently, the police have the footage to prove it."

"Hmmm." Johnny tapped his finger against his

chest. "Then we must be missing something."

Before they could theorise, Julia's phone sung from the sitting room. She left Johnny staring at the wall and grabbed it from her handbag. Barker's picture flashed on the screen.

"Any news?"

"Where are you, Julia?"

"At home."

"Are you alone?"

"Johnny's here." She peered into the dining room to make sure he was not eavesdropping. "He had a somewhat innocent explanation. I'll tell you when I see you."

"It doesn't matter," he said in a rushed voice as what sounded like a car door slammed in the background. "I'm coming back now. Just stay there, and I'll tell you everything when I get back."

"What's happened?"

There was a long pause as Barker started the engine.

"I asked Christie about Brooke's footage," he called, the echo in his voice letting her know he had switched to his car's Bluetooth handsfree function. "He had no idea what I was talking about. He called the station, but they had no idea either. If there is any footage, the police don't have it. Brooke wasn't even a person of interest. She lied to you."

"She was calling my bluff," Julia whispered. "Barker, I need to go."

"Julia, don't do anyth—"

She hung up and put her phone on silent. She hated to block Barker out, but the hospital was a half an hour's drive away, even if he put his foot down. She tossed her phone back into her bag and slung it over her shoulder.

"Johnny, I need to go out," she called into the dining room. "Brooke was lying about her alibi. I think you might have been onto something when you sent me that article."

"Then I'm coming with you," he said as he hurried into the hallway. "I'm not letting you wade into this one alone."

# 15

I t was past nine when Julia pulled up outside *Brooke's Bridal Boutique* on Mulberry Lane, so it was no surprise that the shop, along with all the others, was closed for the day. She stared at the white dresses in the dark window, but they looked ghostly and macabre in the dim glow of the streetlamp.

"Well, she's not here." Julia sighed as she looked down the dark street. "And I have no idea where she lives."

"I could check online?" Johnny pulled his phone from his pocket. "I once found my address on an online directory just by searching my name."

"You searched for yourself online?"

"I was curious." His fingers tapped on the screen. "Do you know if she ever married?"

"Oh." She thought about it for a second. "I have no idea. Try 'Brooke Williams' and see what comes up."

Johnny nodded and began his search. Car headlights dazzled them from behind. A black cab pulled up in front of them. Julia held her breath as she waited for the passenger to climb out. Had fate somehow delivered Brooke to her? The door opened, but it was Roxy. She passed money through the driver's window before slapping the roof with her free hand. Her other hand held a plastic box. Julia pressed her horn, making Johnny and Roxy jump. Roxy walked over, and Julia wound down her window.

"Katie insisted on sending me home with leftovers," Roxy said, indicating the plastic box. "I overheard that DI telling Barker about the body. Was it her?"

"No."

"Oh." Roxy inhaled deeply and nodded. "I'm glad."

"You are?"

"I spent too many years resenting Leah, and it didn't get me anywhere. She made a lot of mistakes, but she didn't deserve to die for them. I had a lot of time to reflect in that interview room. I know there's only a slim chance that she's out there somewhere, but that's better than nothing." Roxy looked over the car at her flat. "Violet is going to be doing back flips in there. What are you doing here?"

"We're looking for Brooke. She lied to me about her alibi."

"Brooke from the bridal shop?" Roxy arched a brow. "Do you think she's behind all this?"

"I need to talk to her first. I don't suppose you know where she lives?"

"Not a clue." Roxy shook her head. "Never spoken to the woman. She never came across as the friendliest. Neither did that lanky son of hers."

"I can't find anything online," Johnny announced. "Looks like we're back to square one. We might have to wait until morning. At least we know she'll be here."

"Or, we just break in." Roxy shrugged as she scrutinised the shop. "She probably has some record of her home address in there."

"And we could check the cameras to see if she

really was here on Tuesday night."

"We're not breaking in!" Julia cried. "There must be another way to find her."

"Like what?"

"Well, I don't know." Julia gripped the steering wheel and looked at the shop. "Someone must know where she lives."

"And how are you going to find them?" Roxy pursed her lips. "C'mon. We sneak in, find what we need, and we leave. I'm not suggesting we trash the place or steal any dresses."

"It's against the law," Julia protested.

"And what if she killed Leah and we find something that pins her to it?" Roxy said. "The police aren't going to care that we broke in if it means we can end this. And if they do care, it's not like Barker doesn't have connections to sort it out."

"And if we find nothing?"

"Then nothing is lost." Roxy opened Julia's car door. "Don't be a killjoy. You know you want to."

Julia decided it was better not to argue. She climbed out of the car and let Roxy store her leftovers on the backseat. She locked the car after Johnny exited, and they gathered on the pavement outside the bridal shop. Like a bad omen, the lights above the sign flickered. Roxy rattled the front doorknob, but it was locked.

"Well, it was worth a shot," Roxy said as she stepped back, her hands on her hips.

"Do we smash the window?" Johnny asked, his cheeks burning bright. "Maybe Julia was right about this being a bad idea."

"Life is a long series of bad decisions," Roxy exclaimed before setting off up the street. "Let's try the back. All the shops have yards."

They walked to the top of the street and turned the corner into the narrow, cobbled alley that ran between Mulberry Lane and the back of the library. Apart from the light spilling from the flats above the shops, the alley was completely dark. The rear of the shops looked the same in the night, so Julia was glad that the boutique had a sign on the back of the building. Roxy rattled the wooden gate, but it was locked like the front.

"It's almost like she doesn't want anyone breaking in," Roxy muttered before stepping back and looking up. "We need to scale the wall. I'll help Julia up, then Johnny can help me up, and then he can climb over."

"Why do I have to climb?" Johnny twitched his glasses.

"Because you're the man."

"I don't have any upper body strength," he shot back. "Don't you remember P.E. at school? I couldn't get up those ropes to save my life. And besides, isn't that sexist?"

"Fine!" Roxy squatted and cupped her hands. "You go over first, Julia can go second, and I'll go last."

Johnny pouted but reluctantly put his foot in Roxy's hands. She grunted and pushed him up enough for him to grab the top of the wall. He panted and flailed, shoes skidding on the crumbly wall. Julia grabbed his other foot and gave him the boost he needed to hoist himself onto the top. Instead of dropping down, which seemed like the logical approach, he jumped like a frog. He landed with a bang that echoed around the stone yard.

"Are you okay?" Julia hissed through the gate.

To her surprise, the gate opened from the inside. Johnny ushered them in as he brushed dust and dirt from his trousers.

"I'm fine." He straightened his jacket. "It was only locked with a latch bolt."

Julia and Roxy walked into the yard. Like the yard behind Julia's café, it was small, with just enough room for the bins and somewhere to get some fresh air in the middle of a busy workday. Also, like Julia's café, double doors were set into the ground, and she guessed they led into a basement similar to the café's.

Roxy peeped through a crack in the wood of the basement doors. "Looks like it's chained from the inside," she said. "We only have one option left."

Roxy walked over to the wall and pulled a piece of stone from the century's old construction. She inspected it as she tossed it up and down in her hand. Seemingly satisfied that it was good enough to break the back window, she walked over to the door and took in a deep lungful of air.

"*Wait!*" Johnny cried when Roxy pulled her arm back to launch. "What if there's a spare key somewhere?"

"Who leaves a spare key in their yard?" Roxy repositioned her feet, her eyes trained on the glass. "Do you, Julia?"

Julia blushed. She thought she had been clever leaving a spare key in her yard, but now that she was about to break into someone's shop, it suddenly felt like an obvious thing to do.

"There's one at the bottom of my hanging basket," she admitted. "Jessie kept losing her keys, so I put it there for emergencies. Johnny's right. It might be worth a look around."

Roxy huffed as she tossed the rock onto the back doorstep. They split up and searched the yard, but there were no hanging baskets or obvious hiding places for keys. Julia yanked on the giant black bin, surprised to see a rock in a plant pot. She picked up the rock and smiled when she saw a shiny key underneath a layer of cobwebs.

"Jackpot," she said as she plucked it out. "Good thinking, Johnny."

"Not just a pretty face." Roxy pinched his cheek. "Although, I was excited to smash something."

Julia shook off the cobwebs before trying it in the lock. It slotted in perfectly, clicking into place like a hand in a glove. She twisted it, and the door gave way.

"We're not a bad team for a school teacher, a journalist, and a café owner," said Roxy, grinning with excitement. "All we need is a talking dog and a Mystery Machine."

Julia pushed on the door. It opened into a basic staff area. The room contained a small kitchenette and a place for two people to eat lunch. Roxy was about to walk right in, but Julia blocked her with her arm.

"Look in the corners," Julia whispered. "Alarm triggers."

"It's not too late to leave, guys," Johnny said, his voice shaking as he looked around the dark yard. "This place is giving me the creeps."

"But we've come this far." Roxy huffed as she scratched her hair. "They could be fake. I've heard of people doing that."

"It's possible," Julia admitted as she scanned the room. "Although, if they are fake, they've put in a lot of detail. I think that's a keypad on the wall."

"There's only one way to find out." Roxy pushed past Julia's arm and walked into the kitchen.

Julia held her breath and waited for the alarm to start blaring. She waited at least ten seconds, but nothing happened. Roxy shrugged with a satisfied smile.

"Nothing!" Roxy cried, tossing her arms out. "I knew it was a dummy. It was so—"

A sudden beeping interrupted Roxy, and the sensors in the corners of the room started to flash red.

"It's a countdown," Julia said. "We need to leave."

"How long do we have until it goes off?"

"About thirty seconds," Julia replied, her heart pounding. "If we're lucky."

Undeterred by the beeping, Roxy ran across the room and tore back the panel for the keypad. She stared at the numbers, but her finger froze over it.

"Do we know her birthday?" she cried over her shoulder. "Or her son's birthday?"

"We need to go," Johnny whined. "I don't like this one bit."

"Try 1234," Julia suggested.

Roxy punched in the numbers, but the beeping continued.

"1111?"

"Nothing," Roxy muttered, the panic rising in her voice. "How long do we have left?"

"Seconds."

"Try 0000," Johnny said, his hands vanishing into his curls. "That's what mine was when I bought it."

Roxy punched in the four digits, and to their collective sighs of relief, the beeping stopped. Roxy hovered on the spot as she looked up at the sensors in the corners of the room, but nothing happened.

"My heart is pounding." Roxy forced a laugh. "That was close."

"*Too* close," Johnny said harshly. "Let's just go! The police are probably already on their way."

"I'm not turning back now." Roxy rolled her eyes. "I just deactivated an alarm system! We're unstoppable right now."

"And what if there's another alarm for the shop?" Johnny began pacing in the yard. "Or worse."

"Worse?"

*"Boobytraps!"*

"It's a bridal boutique, not an *Indiana Jones* movie set!" Roxy opened the door that led into the front. "See. No poison darts or giant boulders. If you want to leave, leave, but I'm not going anywhere until we either confirm or deny Brooke's involvement. I've just been accused of killing Leah, and I'm not stopping until I fully clear my name. Are you in, Julia?"

Julia glanced at Johnny, and then at the gate. It would have been easy to turn back, leave the boutique until morning, and get away with what they had already done, but Roxy's stare compelled Julia to continue. They were both on the same page; they wanted to find Leah.

"I'm in," Julia said, stepping into the kitchen. "Johnny?"

He stopped pacing and stared at her with wide eyes. She offered a reassuring smile. Johnny sighed before hurrying in behind her.

While Roxy began searching the boutique, Julia and Johnny looked around the kitchen. There was a counter with a microwave and a kettle, and a small white fridge underneath. She opened the fridge door, but it was filled with the usual items: a pint of milk, a tub of margarine, some cheese, and yoghurt.

"These guys love soup," Johnny said as he peered into the bin. "There must be ten empty tins of chicken soup in here."

Julia glanced into the open bin, and then at the shelf on the wall above the counter. The shelf held a dozen cans of the same soup and nothing else.

"Maybe they really like that soup." Julia scanned the room. "I don't think there's anything in here."

Julia joined Roxy, digging through a stack of letters, in the boutique. The soft furnishings and the plastic-wrapped dresses felt a lot less inviting in the dark. A car drove past, its headlights dazzling her through the window.

"Cameras," Johnny said when he joined them. "In every corner."

"At least she wasn't lying about having them," Julia replied. "Can we check them?"

Johnny squeezed past Roxy and sat in the chair behind the desk. He wiggled the mouse, and the computer screen lit up. A picture of Brooke and Max standing in front of the shop popped up. Their unsmiling faces stared out at them.

"No password." Johnny smiled as he pulled himself under the desk. "I just need to find the software, and I should be able to check."

"And maybe erase that we were ever here," Roxy muttered as she dropped the papers onto the desk. "Nothing in there." She planted her hands on her hips and looked around the boutique. "There must be a record of her home address in here somewhere."

"I can check the computer," Johnny said as his fingers rapidly tapped the keys. "If she doesn't have a login password, I'm sure she doesn't have them anywhere else."

Roxy dropped to her feet and tried the desk drawers, but they were locked.

"No password on her computer, but she locks her desk," Roxy said as she yanked on the locked doors. "I need to find a key."

Julia joined her behind the desk and looked under everything for a key, but their endeavour was fruitless. She rooted through the pens and pencils in a branded mug, and bright pink paperclips caught her attention.

Julia dug a paperclip out. "Let me try something."

Julia bent one of the paperclips, leaving an end hooked over. Using a pair of scissors as pliers, she squashed down the hook before cutting the clip in half.

She dropped to her knees and forced the clip into the keyhole. With slight pressure, she forced it all the way down before turning it clockwise. With the cut-off piece of metal, she jiggled the wire into the lock, feeling for each pin. Her tongue poked out as she stared into the corner of the room, her eyes focussing on the camera as she felt the last pins of the lock slide back. It clicked, and the tension gave way.

"I lost the key to my jewellery box," Julia explained. "Barker showed me a little trick he picked up during his years on the force."

"Have I ever told you how constantly you impress me?" Roxy planted her hands on Julia's shoulders. "I want to be you when I grow up."

Julia stepped out of the way and let Roxy search through the drawer. She leaned against the back of the chair and watched as Johnny scrolled through a long list of timestamped files.

"Okay, I'm back to Tuesday." Johnny moved closer to the screen. "Every day has its own twenty-four-hour video clip, and it looks like it keeps them on a rolling thirty-day period. I was at Leah's from six until about quarter to nine, so should I start at eight and watch what happens?"

"You were at Leah's?" Roxy looked up, her brow

wrinkled. "Wait, I didn't see you."

"I was upstairs," Johnny muttered, his ears burning bright red.

"Oh," Roxy replied. "*Oh*! Johnny Watson! So, it was *you* I heard snoring? You little rascal!"

"I-I—"

"I didn't think you had it in you." Roxy winked. "We're all adults here, but Leah? *Really*? I never thought she was your type."

"And what is my type?"

"Julia," Roxy offered with another wink. "You're blushing."

"I'm not," Johnny muttered, dropping his head. "Why were you at Leah's, anyway?"

But before Roxy could reply, Johnny clicked on the video file, and it began playing. The screen showed the shop in grainy black and white, the timestamp starting at eight in the evening.

"Well, she wasn't here," Julia said. "Can you fast forward it?"

Johnny hit a key, and the timestamp in the corner zoomed up. The shop remained still, car headlights zooming past every so often.

Johnny exhaled. "Almost midnight." He shook his head. "She wasn't here. She lied to your face."

The video footage reached midnight and stopped. Julia squinted at the screen, sure she had seen movement for the first time.

"Can you go back a couple of seconds?" Julia leaned in closer, her finger tapping on a door in the corner. "I'm sure I just saw that door move."

Johnny scrubbed the video back and played it in normal motion. The door began to open at 11:59:57pm.

"Where's the rest?" Julia urged. "Did you see that?"

"See what?" Roxy stood up and joined Julia behind Johnny. "I didn't see anything."

"Rewind it again. Can you zoom in on that door?"

Johnny did as he was told, and the door filled the screen. It was subtle, but the door cracked open before cutting off.

"Maybe it was a breeze?" Roxy suggested, scratching her head.

"From where?" Julia replied, glancing at the door in the boutique. "It's inside. Johnny, where's the rest of that clip?"

"It will be on the next day." Johnny clicked off the video and scrolled down the list of files. "Wait, it jumps to Thursday. Wednesday isn't here."

Johnny clicked on the next file, which showed Brooke and Max in the shop in the middle of the day. Brooke was vacuuming the carpet, and Max was rearranging the dresses in the window display.

"Why would Wednesday be missing?" Julia asked, her stomach knotting.

"Maybe the file is corrupted?" Johnny clicked off the video and scrolled through the list again. "It looks like Wednesday is the only day that's missing."

"Then someone deleted it." Julia stepped back from the chair and stared into space as her mind whirred. "There's something there Brooke didn't want anyone to see."

"But isn't it more obvious to delete one day?" Roxy asked. "Surely she'd just delete everything?"

"Maybe she didn't think anyone would come looking?" Johnny suggested, his fingers still working the keys. "When we delete things off computers, they're not always as gone as we think they are. Computers cling onto a shadow of a deleted file in case we need to recover it later. If she doesn't put a password on her computer, I doubt she knows that."

"Can you find it?" Julia asked.

"I can try."

Roxy returned to her drawer rummaging while Julia

watched anxiously as Johnny searched through the folders on Brooke's computer.

"I've found it!" Johnny exclaimed. "I didn't think to look in the most obvious place first, but it's right there in her trash folder."

"Oh my God," Roxy whispered. "Julia. I think that drawer was locked for a reason."

Julia investigated the drawer. Her heart stopped when she saw a large, bloody knife wrapped up in a plastic bag.

"The file, Johnny?" Julia urged.

"It's recovering," he replied. "Another forty seconds."

Roxy's covered her mouth with her hand as she began to cry. She backed away from the drawer, stumbling into a dress-wearing mannequin. Julia dove to catch it before it fell, but it slipped through her fingers and clashed with the wall. The head broke free and thudded onto the carpet before rolling away. It hit the front door with a bang and rolled back on itself, its unmoving face staring at them as it settled.

"We need to leave," Julia whispered, her eyes glued to the knife. "The police can deal with this from—"

Before Julia could finish her sentence, careful and crisp footsteps made them all turn and look towards the door that had begun to open on the security footage.

"Someone's here," Roxy said as she tried to straighten up the mannequin. "Julia, what do we do?"

"Ten seconds," Johnny whispered, his eyes fixed on the screen. "It's almost done."

But they didn't have ten seconds. The footsteps grew louder as they came closer.

"Out the back door." Julia turned off the computer screen and spun Johnny's chair around. "We don't have time. We need to leave now."

Johnny nodded and hurried into the kitchen with Roxy. Julia almost followed, but the footsteps stopped, and a door creaked open deep in the shop. Julia's curiosity got the better of her. She mouthed 'go' to Roxy and Johnny before closing the kitchen door.

"Hello?" a voice called out. "Who's there?"

Gulping hard, Julia turned and walked into the middle of the boutique.

# 16

Einstein once said that time was relative; it was the very thought flashing through Julia's mind as she stepped into the middle of the shop. The clock stopped ticking, and Julia's senses heightened. She heard a distant car driving along the top road; she smelled the plastic protecting the dresses; she felt the thick fibre of the carpet under her thin shoes; she tasted the tea she had drunk with Johnny less than half an hour ago at her cottage; and she saw the definite outline of

Brooke standing in the doorway to the cellar.

"Julia?" Brooke stepped out of the shadows. "What are you doing in my shop?"

Julia gulped. Brooke's usual black pencil skirt and blazer combination had been swapped for dark blue jeans, a black turtleneck shirt, and a fitted leather jacket. In her panic, all Julia could think about was how warm Brooke must feel swathed in leather.

"I wanted to speak to you," Julia said, her voice stronger than she had expected. "It's urgent."

"How did you get in here?" Brooke's eyes danced to the disembodied plastic head on the carpet. "Did I leave the door unlocked?"

"I broke in."

"You broke in?" Brooke arched a brow.

"Technically."

"You either did, or you didn't."

"I found the backdoor key behind the bin in the yard," Julia confessed.

Brooke's head tilted. She looked as though she was remembering the existence of her spare key and mentally berating herself for leaving it where she had.

"I see." Brooke nodded carefully as she took another step into the shop, the light from the lamppost outside washing her in a hazy glow. "And I suppose you guessed the alarm code? I've been meaning to change that."

"It was a third attempt." Julia glanced at the kitchen door, which was thankfully still closed. "But I got it in the end."

Brooke's thin lips tightened as her eyes narrowed on Julia. She looked like a predator trying to decide what to do with her latest catch.

"What could be so urgent that it couldn't wait until morning?" Brooke forced interest into her flat voice. "Something tells me it's not about the dress you tried on earlier today."

"I know you lied to me about the security footage."

Brooke's expression barely cracked.

"And I know the police didn't come to talk to you about your history with Leah." Julia stiffened her spine as she gulped down her fear. "You were calling my bluff. In fact, trying to get me to buy the dress was part of your charade. You wanted me to think you had nothing to hide."

Brooke nodded as she took in the information. Her eyes drifted to the open desk drawer, and the corners of her lips pricked up into a half-smile that vanished as quickly as it had appeared.

"So, you didn't believe me?"

"I had no reason to think you were lying," Julia said, "but I wanted to double check. I'm glad I did."

"And you came here to confront me?"

"I came here to find out where you lived." Julia took a small step back when she noticed that Brooke had almost closed the gap between them. "I thought you might have a record of your home address."

"Did you find what you were looking for?"

"I found the footage." Julia glanced back at the desk, wishing she had closed the drawer. "I know you lied about being here on the night Leah disappeared, and I know you deleted the footage after midnight."

Brooke almost looked impressed that Julia had figured out so much.

"So, I lied about where I was." Brooke shrugged as she folded her arms, the old leather groaning. "Hardly a motive for killing Leah."

"Who said anything about killing Leah?"

Brooke's lips parted, but she stopped and grinned.

"Checkmate." Brooke chuckled as she shook her head. "I knew you were trouble from the moment you turned up at my shop with *that* woman. You should have let me beat her to death then and there."

"I found the knife." Julia gulped. "The knife covered in blood that you hid in your locked drawer."

"And you think I murdered Leah?"

"Didn't you?"

Brooke considered her response for a moment, her icy gaze unwavering.

"They were right about you being a little busybody." Brooke sighed as she rubbed between her eyes. "Why did you have to get involved? It had nothing to do with you."

"Leah was my friend."

"Then you need to pick your friends more wisely." Brooke's eyes snapped onto Julia. "You say you know what she did to my father, and yet you still care enough about her to break into my shop to uncover my lie? I don't know if you're stupid, or if I should admire your conviction."

"I just want the truth."

"The *truth*?" Brooke's eyes glazed over. "If Leah had told the truth at the trial, my life would have turned out very differently."

"I'm sorry about your father."

"Are you?" Brooke cried. "Was he your teacher at Hollins?"

"For a time. I didn't take drama as a GCSE subject, but he taught me in my early years."

"And what was your assessment of him?" Brooke

cocked her head back. "Be honest."

Julia's feet felt glued to the spot as dread tightened every muscle.

"I liked him," Julia said carefully. "Everyone did. He was funny and sweet."

A soft smile crossed Brooke's face for a second before the icy glare returned.

"A lot of people shared that opinion." Brooke's jaw tightened. She looked like she was biting back tears. "He was a good man, but bad things happen to good people, don't they? Do you know what it's like to lose a parent?"

"I do."

"Then you know the void their absence leaves behind." Brooke's lashes fluttered as she stared into the distance. "How did they die?"

"Cancer."

"*Ha!*" Brooke shook her head. "Then nature decided it was their time to go. Don't you think that makes it easier?"

"I was twelve."

"Then you've had longer to get over it." Brooke's face drained of colour. "My father didn't have the luxury of natural selection. Leah robbed him of his reputation, making his life impossible, so he ended it.

He was the sunshine in my life, my best friend. I haven't felt that light in over twenty years. Do you know how that feels?"

Julia understood perfectly, but Brooke was not in the frame of mind to accept empathy. Julia might have had longer to miss her mother, but the void had yet to close. Julia didn't think it ever would, not completely. Still, she shook her head, conceding.

"I thought things would get easier with time," Brooke continued. "I waited for the colour to return to my life. I sought love and had a child, but it barely changed things. My life and heart have been grey since the day he died, all because of Leah. She was the cancer that ruined my family." Brooke swallowed hard before taking another step forward. "Are you a Christian woman, Julia?"

"I don't know."

"So, you don't believe in Heaven?"

"I don't know that either."

"Well, I do." Brooke's lips tightened. "I turned to God when my father left me. I thought I would find some solace in religion. I didn't, but I took the Bible to heart. It gave me some strength to know that my father was in Heaven waiting for me. Knowing I will one day join him is what gets me out of bed in the morning."

Julia understood grieving, but Brooke had ventured beyond that. Her grief had developed into an obsession, and it had clouded her vision. Julia wanted to remind her that she had a son to live for, but she bit her tongue.

"Heaven is where good people go when they die," Brooke explained. "There's another place for the bad people."

"Hell."

"Exactly." Brooke smirked. "Where do you think you'll end up?"

The question made Julia quiver. She shrugged, not wanting to feed into Brooke's game.

"Well, are you a good woman, or a bad woman?"

"I don't think it's that simple."

"Isn't it?" Brooke snapped. "Our actions and intentions determine where we go in the next life. I have no doubt that I will be reunited with my father. No doubt at all. I have sinned, as we all have, but God can see through to our hearts. The Bible teaches us 'an eye for an eye.' In this case, it's a life for a life."

"And Jesus told us to turn the other cheek," Julia reminded Brooke. "If someone asks for your shirt, you give them your coat as well. You don't beat evil with evil, you rise above it."

"Rise above it?" Brooke snorted. "We're not talking about a coat, we're talking about my father's life. A life ruined by a silly girl. It's a simple equation. Her actions directly led to my father's death, so she got what she deserved."

"And what did she get?" The question dried out Julia's throat. "Did you kill Leah?"

Brooke's eyes twinkled as the corners of her lips darted up; she was enjoying every second.

"I did," Brooke whispered, her head moving closer to Julia. "And I'd do it again if I could."

Julia's heart dropped. The last light of hope she had been clinging to had just been snuffed out before her. She clenched her fists in disbelief as tears welled.

"How did you kill her?"

"I stabbed her," Brooke said in a matter-of-fact voice. "I went to her house, and I stabbed her."

"And her body?"

"I hid it."

"Where?"

Brooke considered her response for a long, dragged out minute.

"I took her out into the fields, I dug a hole, and I dumped her. You'll never find her. I don't think I could retrace my steps even if I wanted to."

"And did it work?"

"Excuse me?"

"Did it fix you?" Julia's heart thumped in her chest. "I don't think it did. That rage and misery will swirl around in you until the day you die. You went through one of the worst things a person can go through. I sympathise with that, I really do, but Leah wasn't the thing holding you back from moving on. You've had twenty years to find her and kill her, and I don't doubt you would have succeeded if you had wanted to. The problems you have go much deeper than one person. It's ingrained within you. What Leah said about your father was wrong, but she didn't kill him. He made that choice. And Leah didn't force you to fester in your grief for this long. That was also your choice. This has nothing to do with Leah; this is about you."

Brooke's eyes widened. A car drove past the shop, its headlights shining through the window, but Brooke didn't blink. Julia knew she had just told her what she had always known, and she doubted Brooke was going to let her get away with it.

"How *dare* you!" Brooke hissed. "What do *you* know?"

"I know that if you let a broken bone heal, it becomes the strongest part of the bone, but if you ignore the break and just keep splitting it apart before it can mend, it's going to make things so much worse. You never allowed yourself to heal because it's easier to stay stuck in that dark place. The darkness becomes a comfort, a security blanket. It becomes the only familiar feeling you have, so you stay stuck under that blanket. Change is a test, and you didn't want to be tested. It became easier for you to pin all your issues on the woman you perceived to have ruined your entire life, and what has that made you?" Julia waited for Brooke to respond, but her stunned expression said it all. "You're a murderer, and you'll have to live with that until you take your dying breath."

"Maybe you're right," Brooke said as she reached into her leather jacket, "but you're not going to be around to find out. It's time for *you* to take your dying breath."

Brooke pulled a large knife from her jacket. It glittered as another car drove past the window. Julia took another step back, but Brooke copied the motion, closing the gap between them even more. Julia knew it would take hardly any effort at all for Brooke to stab her.

Before that could happen, the staff room door crashed open, knocking the headless mannequin over.

The confusion allowed Julia to back away from Brooke, who was transfixed by Roxy running into the shop with the microwave over her head. A deep, rasping scream filled the shop as Roxy dumped the microwave on Brooke. Brooke crumpled under its weight and landed on the floor with a thud. The knife fell away from her grasp. Julia kicked it, and it slid under the rack of dresses.

"Have I killed her?" Roxy cried as she backed away.

Julia knelt and pressed her fingers against Brooke's neck.

"She has a pulse," Julia said. "I think you've just knocked her out. You took your time to make your entrance."

"I didn't expect her to pull out a knife!" Roxy stepped back and clamped both hands against her head. "How were you so calm?"

"I knew you'd be listening to every word." Julia allowed herself a sigh of relief. "I'm assuming you heard her confession?"

Roxy nodded, eyes dropping to the floor. Julia wanted to hug her, but the kitchen door burst open again, and Johnny ran in, red-faced. Barker and DI Christie followed. Barker's relief was obvious the moment his eyes landed on Julia.

"I've been trying to call you!" Barker's gaze drifted to Brooke on the floor. "A microwave?"

"It was a microwave or a tin of soup," Roxy said. "I didn't think chicken soup would be enough to stop that madwoman stabbing Julia."

"*Stabbing*?" Barker echoed, clamping his eyes shut. "This is why I didn't want you rushing into things without me."

"She didn't stab me," Julia said with a sheepish smile. "And she confessed to everything."

"She did?" Christie asked. "Oh, I could cry with happiness right now. What did she do?"

"She murdered Leah and buried her body," Julia croaked. "She said she'd never reveal where she hid her."

"We'll get it out of her," Christie said confidently as he pulled his phone from his pocket. "I need to call this in. Forensics are going to rip this place apart."

"The deleted video footage!" Johnny exclaimed, clicking his fingers together as she hurried to the computer. "It might—"

"You can't touch that!" Christie cried. "This is a crime scene."

"Our prints are all over everything already," Julia

said. "We broke in."

Johnny turned the computer on again. The trash can folder illuminated the screen, but it was empty. Johnny clicked back into the camera software. The lost clip had been restored. He double clicked on it, and the grainy video jumped up onto the screen, picking up where the last clip had ended.

The door opened, and a shadowy woman in nothing more than a t-shirt ran into the dark shop, limping and clutching her hand. Julia knew exactly who she was despite the poor quality.

"That's Leah," Johnny said.

They continued to watch, and a second figure burst in. This one was tall and lanky, with shaggy black hair.

"Max," Julia muttered. "Brooke's son."

Max dove on Leah. He dragged her back towards the door, her legs and arms flailing. They both vanished into the darkness, and the door slammed behind them. They waited for something else to occur, but the shop looked as though nothing had happened. Johnny fast forwarded the clip, but it contained no other movement until Brooke arrived to open the shop at eight in the morning. Max followed her in, his eyes darting right up into the camera.

"I don't understand," Roxy said, her brows tight.

"That's not what Brooke said."

Brooke groaned on the floor. Before anyone could do or say anything, Julia darted for the cellar door.

"*Julia!*" Barker cried, running after her. "*Wait!*"

Julia tore open the door and took the stone steps two at a time into the dark, cold cellar. While her eyes were adjusting, she heard chains rustling on the far side of the room. Without a second thought, she ran towards the sound. The double doors to the yard outside world flew open, letting in the light of the moon. Julia squinted, catching a glimpse of Max as he darted up the wooden steps to the doors. Without glancing back, he dashed into the yard. Julia ran after him, scrambling up the wooden ladder.

She emerged into the yard to find the back gate still swinging. She barrelled through it in time to see Max emerging at the top of the street just as a blaring police car sped towards Mulberry Lane. The two collided with a thud, sending Max up into the air. Tyres screeched to a halt out of view. Julia pressed her hand against her mouth.

"*Julia!*" Barker's voice echoed from the cellar. "You need to see this."

In a daze from what she had witnessed, Julia turned around and walked back into the yard. She climbed carefully down the ladder into the cellar, which was now illuminated by a single bulb hanging from the beams. The light revealed a sewing machine and racks of more plastic wrapped dresses. Everyone stood crowded around something in the corner.

"A police car just hit Max," Julia said calmly. "Someone needs to call an ambulance."

"Two are already on the way," Roxy said as she backed away from the corner. "I can't believe it."

Julia was about to ask what Roxy couldn't believe, but the crowd shifted enough for her to see. Leah was slumped in the corner, her left wrist handcuffed to a pipe. Her head lolled against her shoulder, and her eyes were clamped shut, but her chest softly rose and fell under a filthy white t-shirt that was several sizes too big.

"She's alive," Julia mumbled. "Leah's alive."

# 17

J ulia woke with a start, banging her head on the wall behind her. She found herself sitting upright in a chair, with her arms folded tightly across her body. The scent of strong disinfectant and the sound of muffled machine beeps reminded her she was in a hospital; it took a moment to remember why.

Jumping up, she looked through the window of the room she had fallen asleep outside of. Leah was propped up in bed in a blue gown with white sheets neatly tucked around her. Her bruised and scratched arms were by her sides, and one hand had a thick bandage around it. Wires and tubes trailed off her, but otherwise, she looked like she was taking a peaceful nap. Julia scanned the corridor; she had no idea what time it was in the windowless depths of the hospital. Her panic eased when Barker rounded the corner carrying two cups in his hands.

"Morning," he said, passing her one of the cups.

"Is it?"

"The sun has just risen. I thought you might need a strong coffee after last night."

Julia slurped the hot coffee—the caffeine was just what she required. After leaving the boutique the night before, she, Roxy, and Johnny had been whisked straight to the station to give separate statements about the events leading up to finding Leah. The police had kept them until the early hours of the morning before releasing them. They didn't so much as thank them for cracking the case, and they even had the nerve to say that they wouldn't be charging them with breaking and entering on 'this occasion,' while reminding them that calling 999 was free. Julia drove straight to the hospital to see Leah, but her friend had still been unconscious when she arrived. Julia remembered sitting in the chair, but not falling asleep.

"Brooke and Max have been taken to another hospital," Barker explained as Julia continued to stare into space as her mind woke up. "They're under constant supervision. Brooke's awake, but Max was still in surgery the last I heard. The car hit him pretty bad."

"Will he survive?"

"They think so."

"Good."

"Is it?"

"There's been enough death." Julia sipped her coffee and turned to the window. "They both need to face justice for what they've done."

"And we still don't know exactly what happened." Barker sighed before stifling a yawn. He looked like he hadn't slept. "Brooke isn't saying a word, so we won't know anything until Leah wakes up and gives us her version of events."

"I'm just glad she's alive." Julia gazed into the room. "She looks so weak."

They turned when a doctor turned the corner. She was looking over notes attached to a clipboard, lost in her thoughts. She smiled sympathetically when she noticed them.

"You're awake." The doctor held out a hand to

Julia. "I'm Doctor Maryam Khan. I don't usually like people sleeping in the corridors, but the police told me what you went through, so I let it slide." She smiled again, the corners of her eyes crinkling. "It's a good job you found her when you did."

"Is there any news?" Julia glanced at Leah. "What's happened to her?"

"I've just been looking over her bloodwork and x-rays." Doctor Khan flipped through the papers. "There's the deep cut on her hand, of course, which she's fortunate isn't severely infected, and surface abrasions and contusions. However, there are no signs of internal trauma. She does have a high concentration of diphenhydramine hydrochloride in her blood."

"What's that?"

"A common antihistamine found in over-the-counter sleeping pills." Doctor Khan dropped the clipboard to her side and exhaled. "We're well into overdose territory. In my professional opinion, she's been fed large amounts of the medication."

"Is it lethal?"

"It can be." Doctor Khan tipped her head from side to side. "But I'm confident she'll live. She's just asleep right now. Her blood pressure is a little low, and she might be irritable or nauseous when she wakes up, but that's about it. We've given her a vitamin and fluids intravenous to build her back up. We could force her out of this sleep with some adrenaline shots, but I don't think that's necessary. From the sounds of it, she needs the rest."

Doctor Khan entered the room. They watched as she checked the readings on the machines while scribbling on the clipboard. When she was satisfied, she bowed out of the room and left them to continue observing Leah.

"Sleeping pills." Julia shook her head as she rubbed her temples. "Remember when we saw Max smoking in front of the shop the day after Leah was taken? He had a bag from the pharmacy in his hand. They've had her chained up in that basement while pumping her full of pills to keep her docile. I was there yesterday afternoon. If I'd just—"

"Seen through the floor?" Barker wrapped his arm around her. "There was no way you could have known."

"Max came up those cellar stairs," Julia said as she leaned her head against his shoulder. "He poured us champagne and then vanished like nothing was going on."

"There's clearly a lot we have yet to learn."

It took hours for them to learn the truth. Julia and

Barker hung around outside the room while doctors and nurses came and went. The police showed up more than once to get a statement from Leah but left disappointed when they saw she was still asleep.

Leah's eyelids finally started fluttering at two in the afternoon, while Julia and Barker ate tuna and cucumber sandwiches bought from the hospital shop. Julia ditched her sandwich on the chair and quickly swallowed the food in her mouth.

"*Doctor?*" Julia called down the corridor. "Anyone? She's waking up."

Doctor Khan rounded the corner and ran towards them, quickly followed by two nurses. Julia and Barker stepped back and watched as Leah came around from her drug-induced sleep. When Leah looked through the window and locked eyes with Julia, both women began to cry.

It took twenty minutes for Doctor Khan to finish performing her tests on Leah. When she was done, she told Julia she could have five minutes with Leah, but no more because the patient was still very frail. Julia stood in the doorway and stared at Leah; it was like staring at a ghost.

"Welcome back," Julia said.

"What day is it?" Leah croaked. "The doctor told

me that you found me."

"I wouldn't have stopped until I did." Julia rushed over to Leah's side and pulled up a chair. She took Leah's hand in hers. "It's Saturday morning. You've been gone all week."

"Is that all?" Leah's face crinkled. "I feel like I was down there for weeks. He kept feeding me cold chicken soup with white bits floating in it. The doctor said I've been drugged with sleeping pills, but I already suspected as much." Leah paused to cough, which rattled deep in her lungs. "It was so cold down there. Is the heatwave over?"

"No." Julia rubbed Leah's hand with her thumb. "It's still hotter than hell out there." She laughed before swallowing hard. "What happened to you, Leah? Brooke said she came to your house and killed you. She told me she buried you in a field."

"That's what she told me she was going to do." Leah frowned. "She said it every chance she got. I started to wish she would just get it over with. I didn't think I'd ever get out from there."

"What happened the night she took you?"

"She didn't." Leah licked her dry, cracked lips. "Max took me. I was at my cottage with, uh, with—"

"I know about Johnny," Julia said, squeezing her

hand. "And Roxy. And everything else that happened before you left Peridale."

Leah nodded, her eyes darting away from Julia. She seemed embarrassed.

"After Brooke attacked me at the shop, I walked around Peridale for hours," Leah continued. "I decided I was going to go home, pack my things, and never come back. I felt like a fool for returning. I thought I'd moved on from my past, but nobody else had—not that I can blame them." She paused and bit the edge of her lip. "I got home to pack up my car, but Johnny turned up. He was shouting and screaming, and I just broke down. One thing led to another, and we ended up in bed. I must have fallen asleep. I woke up to Roxy banging on the door. I tried to get rid of her. I didn't want her to catch me with Johnny, so I brushed her off. She deserved an explanation, but I wasn't in a place to give it to her. She left. I promised myself I'd talk to her the next day when things weren't as crazy. I went into the kitchen to start making dinner. I was going to surprise Johnny with it." She smiled. "Did you know I always had a crush on him growing up?"

"I didn't."

"Well, I did." Leah laughed. "I fancied the pants off him, but then my life became crazy, and I used him like

I used everyone else. I was a mess."

"I've heard the stories."

"I was a kid." Leah sighed and squeezed her eyes shut. "I went through something no kid should ever have to." She inhaled deeply. "I started making dinner, and then there was another knock at the door. I thought it was Roxy again. I answered it, and it was a tall man with his back to me. I asked him who he was, but he didn't speak. When he turned around, he had a knife in his hands. I didn't recognise him as the kid from the bridal shop at first. He lunged at me with the knife. I could see it in his eyes, he was going for the kill. He slashed open my hand, and then I tripped over the hallway carpet—that damn ugly carpet. I always told my mum I hated it. In that moment, I thought I was about to join her wherever she was so I could tell her to her face. I fell into the side table. I struggled against him, but he hit me with that awful lamp. I remember seeing the carpet before I hit the floor, and then I woke up in a car. My clothes were gone, and I was in a baggy white t-shirt. I realised it was the t-shirt he had been wearing. I thought I was driving to my death. I was in and out. I remember him carrying me, and then I was in the basement. I tried to escape, but I was woozy from the concussion. He dragged me back down there and chained me up to a pipe."

Julia fought back her tears as she listened to Leah's story, giving her friend an encouraging nod.

"He was sitting on a chair staring at me," Leah continued. "I begged him to let me go. My hand was bleeding really bad. He wrapped it up with an old rag. He said he was going to kill me, but I could tell he couldn't do it. He was just a kid. I told him I wouldn't say anything if he let me go. I even offered him money, and he looked like he was considering it, but he kept snapping back to being angry at me. He kept repeating the same words over and over. 'You ruined my life. You ruined my life.' He kept blaming me for how distant his mother was with him. He told me it was my fault she never loved him. It was my fault that he had the upbringing he had. I ruined his family and took it from him before he was even born. He had so much rage, so much hurt."

Leah paused and reached out for a cup of water on the side table. Julia helped her steady the cup against her lips so she could take a sip.

"Thank you." Leah dabbed at her wet lips. "We were down there for hours, and then he disappeared. I thought I was going to freeze to death. The stone was so cold. I don't know how many hours it was before he came back. I had no way of knowing if it was night or day. When he returned, he had the soup. I ate it because I was hungry, and then I fell asleep. I thought I was just exhausted. It took me a couple of rounds with the soup to realise what was going on."

"And Brooke?"

"She didn't turn up until later. I think she found me by accident. She screamed and asked what I was doing there. Max ran in and dragged her out. He must have explained what he'd done because when she came back, she had a smile on her face. It's the smile you have when you catch a fly you've been chasing around your house for hours. She showed me a missing poster, and she promised that no one would find me. That's when she started telling me that she was going to kill me. Max seemed crazy, but Brooke was completely unhinged. She kept talking over every detail of her dad's trial. She wouldn't listen to me.

"They took it in turns to watch over me. I started to crave the cold soup because it meant I would be able to get away from them staring. I was always disappointed when I woke up. I just wanted to be up there with my mum. I felt like Max wanted to put an end to things, but Brooke was enjoying it. The last thing I remember before waking up in here was them both down in the cellar with me. We all heard a bang, and then she went upstairs. We listened for what felt like a lifetime. We heard another bang, and that's when Max lost it. He told me he was going to take me away and 'end things.' He didn't even try to hide the sleeping pills that time. He crushed up half a packet into the soup and forced it down my throat. And then I woke up in here."

Julia couldn't summon any words. She couldn't imagine a person going through such a horrific ordeal and living to tell the tale. Her mind was swimming with questions, but one stuck out, blaring like a siren.

"Why?" Julia asked. "Why did you lie about Brooke's father?"

"*Lie?*" Leah scrunched up her face and pulled her hand away. "You think I lied too?"

"But the trial, and—"

"Who were they going to believe?" Leah interrupted, anger in her voice. "A sixteen-year-old girl, or a well-loved teacher with more charisma than you could shake a stick at? Even my own mother didn't believe me. I wish I'd never told anyone what he did to me, but I didn't know what else to do. It didn't even cross my mind that people would think I was lying. I was the perfect student. What would I gain from lying?"

Leah paused as if waiting for Julia to answer. Though Julia had asked herself the same question more than once, she hadn't been able to come up with an answer. She shrugged helplessly.

"I loved his drama classes," Leah said. "It was my favourite subject, and he was my favourite teacher. It was the one place in school where I didn't have to be perfect. I could let go and express myself. When he asked me to stay behind and help photocopy scripts, I jumped at the chance. I stayed behind every Friday. I didn't realise it at first, but he was grooming me. He started buying me things. Little things at first. A chocolate bar here, and a can of pop there, but then it turned into perfume and make-up. I just thought he was being nice to me. I was always naïve, but he should have known better. It was just before the Christmas break when he tried to kiss me. I freaked out and ran. I bumped into Mrs Samson from the science department, and I told her. She believed me instantly and took me to the headmaster's office, but he was less supportive. He asked if I was sure. Can you believe that? It was a different time back then, but it's not an excuse. If I'd said it today, people might have believed me. Things are different now, but I wasn't so lucky back then. Regardless, he called the police, and they treated me a little better, though but I was held at arm's length like I was suspected of something."

Doctor Khan appeared in the doorway, but Julia held up five fingers and shook her head. The doctor understood that she needed longer and bowed out of the room.

"Go on," Julia urged. "What happened next?"

"Gary told them I'd tried to kiss him and that I was upset that he rejected me," Leah continued. "It made sense. I couldn't prove all the things he'd bought me. I felt completely alone. Then the trial happened, and he was found not guilty. I couldn't believe it. I'd exposed myself and told the truth, and a bunch of adults told me I was a manipulative liar. You knew me back then, Julia. I was anything but. I was just a girl."

"I know." Julia squeezed her hand.

"My life spiralled out of control after that. My mother tried to make me forget things. She took me on holiday and acted like it would fix everything. She couldn't understand why it didn't work when we got back to Peridale. 'Stop being a silly little girl, Leah', she'd say. I stopped protesting. The entire world didn't believe me, and I knew they never would, so I crashed and burned. I became a self-fulfilling prophecy. They called me a manipulative liar, and I became one. It all exploded at Roxy's birthday party. She told me she was gay, and—I'm guessing you know what I did to her?"

Julia nodded.

"I have no idea why." Leah blinked, and tears formed on her lashes. "Having that power over her gave me a rush. I knew it was wrong, but it made me feel like I was in control of something for once. After the trial, it was like I had someone deep within, scratching to get out. She came out that night. The bitter, evil version of Leah that I became was born then. I didn't notice the shift at the time, but after years of expensive therapy, it all goes back to that night.

"And it wasn't just Roxy, it was Johnny too. He was so sweet, and I used him. Before Mr Williams tried to kiss me, I was summoning the courage to ask Johnny out, but I was so shy. The new version of me wasn't shy. I jumped straight to the end result, and then I ignored him until I left Peridale. I didn't want him to get sucked into my vortex. I wish I'd done the same with Roxy, but we were feeding off each other's energies. I was draining her. I hated myself, but I couldn't stop the self-sabotage. I felt like I was driving down a hill in a speeding car and the brakes had been cut. I didn't fully crash until I met Craig.

"We both wanted an escape, so we took it. I never meant to ruin a wedding, but, at the time, I honestly didn't care. We ran away, and for the first time in years, I felt needed and loved. We only had each other to depend on. It was nice, for a time. I thought I was on the right path, but that bitterness didn't go away. I ruined our marriage like I ruined everything else, and I ran again. I started a new life, and I remarried, but it ended just as badly. I remember being twenty-nine, sitting on a park bench with all my possessions in a single, black bag. It was near Christmas, and it was raining. I was drinking straight from a bottle of wine. I must have looked a state. A man walked past and tossed a pound coin at my feet. I felt so pathetic that I started laughing uncontrollably."

"You could have come home," Julia urged. "You could have come to me."

"You wouldn't have wanted me then." Leah smiled. "I was ready to change my life, but I wasn't there. I started to sort my life out the next day. I moved to York, and I found myself a flat. I got a job as a wedding planner's assistant. It was the last thing I wanted to do, but it was the only job that got back to me after over thirty interviews. It turned out I was quite good at it, and the money was decent. Enough to pay for the best therapists. I realised I had serious issues, and I needed to sort them out. It took months for me to find the right person, but when I did, I let her dig deep to my core and unpick me. She reminded me about who I was before I became that person. I could never be that naïve girl again, but I didn't have to keep self-destructing for the rest of my life.

"I started my own wedding planning business. Having that focus saved me. I kept up with the therapy for years until I had another epiphany. I was in a supermarket buying dinner for one, and a voice dropped into my head and said 'Leah, it's okay to forgive yourself.' I had never stopped beating myself up about what I had done to others. I thought about reaching out so many times, but I honestly thought people would have moved on. I didn't come back to Peridale to stir things up again. I thought people would have figured things out for themselves after the letter."

"What letter?"

"Gary's suicide note." Leah inhaled deeply before looking up to the ceiling. "Gary visited my mother on the day he killed himself and gave her a letter to pass to me. I'd already moved away, and I wasn't speaking to Mum at the time. She was so ashamed of me for running off with Craig. I didn't find out about the note until she got sick this year."

"What did it say?"

"It was an apology." A tear ran down Leah's cheek. "And a confession. He admitted what he had done to me, and he apologised. That's all I ever wanted. I didn't want the man to die." Leah wiped away the tear with a shaky hand. "Mum kept the letter all those years. She didn't want to disrupt my life. She thought me moving away was a sign I'd mentally moved on. It would have been nice to have had that validation. That letter was part of the reason I came back to Peridale. I had the letter in front of me the night that I drank wine and decided I was moving into Mum's house. It felt like permission. I assumed everyone else knew he'd confessed, but it turns out everyone's feelings towards me had been frozen where they were on the day I left."

Leah's fingers pulled at the perfect sheets as more tears clouded her eyes.

"I tried to tell Brooke and Max about the letter, but they didn't believe me. Why would they? I can't blame them for wanting me to suffer. Part of me felt like it was my karma for how I treated everyone in the wake of the trial."

"Nobody deserves this." Julia squeezed Leah's uninjured hand hard. "For the first time since you came back to Peridale, I understand you. I'm not going to lie and say I didn't judge you based on other people's stories, but now I can see the truth, and I'm so sorry."

Leah nodded as more tears rolled down her face. The door opened, and Doctor Khan gestured for Julia to leave; she had stayed way over her five minutes.

"She needs rest," Doctor Khan said gently, "and so do you. Go home. We'll take good care of her."

Julia reluctantly let go of Leah's hand. She kissed her on the forehead before walking towards the door.

"There's a box in my bedroom," Leah called. "A wooden box with a lotus carving. The letter is in there if you need proof."

"I believe you, Leah." Julia looked her in the eyes. "I'll be back later."

Leaving Leah in Doctor Khan's capable hands, Julia left the hospital with Barker. As they walked across the car park to Barker's car, she spotted Johnny and Roxy heading to the entrance, each with a bunch of flowers. They didn't notice her, and she didn't attract their attention; they needed their own healing moments with Leah. The flowers were a good sign they were ready for it.

"The body I viewed last night," Julia said when she was in Barker's car. "Did they find out who she was?"

"Milly Brindle." Barker started the engine after securing his seatbelt. "She was a forty-three-year-old homeless woman. Died of a drug overdose. Her brother identified her this morning."

Julia nodded, glad the woman had someone who was going to miss and remember her.

"Let's go home," Julia said, looking fondly at Barker.

They drove back to Peridale. Julia considered stopping to check the wooden lotus box with Gary's letter, but she decided against it. She believed every word Leah had told her, and that was all that mattered.

# 18

*Two Weeks Later*

The heatwave finally broke when September arrived, and by Julia's birthday, the crispness in the air signalled that autumn was around the corner.

"Thirty-nine!" Dot exclaimed as they sat around Julia's dining table, eating birthday cake. "Do you feel old?"

"I didn't until you reminded me."

"Age is just a number, dear." Dot pushed at her

curls before sipping champagne. "You're as old as you feel."

"How old do you feel, Gran?" Sue asked as she peered at the twins, sound asleep in their pram.

"Oh, about twenty-five?" Dot waved her hand. "Twenty-six?"

"And you don't look a day over eighty-four!" Barker lifted his champagne flute.

"I *am* eighty-four." Dot pursed her lips as she wriggled her brooch. "Did you get everything you wanted for your birthday?"

Julia looked at the small pile of gifts at the end of the table. A new dressing gown and slippers from Dot, a hair curler that she would never use from Sue, and a brand-new electric mixer for the café from Barker. She smiled and nodded, but the one thing she craved was still in Australia and wouldn't be home for another week.

"Good!" Dot announced before reaching into her bag to pull out a stack of wedding magazines. "Because we only have two months to plan this wedding! Sue, Katie, and I have agreed we will help you organise the whole thing free of charge. I know Leah has probably offered to continue planning, but after everything she went through, we don't want to overload her, do we?"

"That's so kind of you, Gran," Julia said, "but I'll have to decline your services."

"*Decline?*" Dot cried as she dropped the stack onto the table. "Two months, Julia! *Two!* How do you think you're going to plan a wedding in two months?"

"I'm not."

"*What?*" Sue spat, choking on her drink. "You've called the wedding off?"

"No." Julia shook her head as she glanced at Barker. "We've already planned everything."

"P-planned *everything?*" Dot wrinkled her nose. "In the two weeks since you stopped hunting for Leah like a sniffer dog?"

"We did it together," Barker jumped in. "It was quite easy, actually."

"*Easy?*" Dot cried. "Oh, no! This is worse than I feared. If it was easy, dear, you've done it wrong."

"We did it exactly as we wanted to do it." Julia reached out and gripped Barker's hand. "We're having a simple village wedding."

Dot looked like she was about to pass out, but there was a knock at the door before she could protest. Julia hurried out and answered the door to Roxy and Johnny.

"*Happy Birthday!*" they announced together.

Roxy handed over a wrapped bottle of what Julia assumed was wine, and Johnny passed her a card. They both kissed her on the cheek as they let themselves in. Johnny was holding a large bouquet of red roses.

"Beautiful flowers," Julia said.

"They're not for you." Johnny fiddled with his glasses, smiling awkwardly. "They're for Leah."

"Besotted, I tell you!" Roxy cried, shaking her head as she walked into the dining room. "I'd feel sick if I wasn't so happy for him."

Julia could barely contain her smile. She knew Leah and Johnny had been seeing each other, but to see a visual representation of their blossoming love in the flowers turned her into something of a mushy mess.

"It's going good between you?" Julia asked, holding back in the hallway with Johnny.

"I think so," he replied, his cheeks reddening. "I know a lot has happened, but it feels right. Now that things have calmed down, I'm going to ask her to be my girlfriend. If Craig and Heidi are giving it another go after everything they've been through, I don't see why I can't try with Leah. Do you think she'll want to?"

Julia bit into her lip. She wanted to tell Johnny that Leah had already visited that morning to give her a birthday card and had mentioned that she was going to ask Johnny to make their relationship official.

"I have a good feeling." Julia winked. "I'm really happy for you."

"I'm happy for me too. Things seem to be looking up. I've even been promoted at work. The editor called me into a meeting, and I thought he was going to either fire me or announce more budget cuts. It turns out, he's retiring, and he wants me to take his job. You're now looking at the brand-new editor of *The Peridale Post*."

"That's wonderful news!"

"It's everything I ever wanted."

"Do you have time for birthday cake before you rush off, Romeo?"

"Only if you baked it."

"Of course."

"Then I'll have a tiny slice." Johnny smiled. He set off towards the dining room before stopping and looking down. He turned back to Julia with a smile. "Thank you, Julia."

"What for?"

"For being a good friend."

He headed into the dining room, and Julia was about to follow him, but there was another knock at the door. She turned, immediately recognising the platinum hair through the frosted glass. Julia opened the door to Katie, who was holding baby Vinnie. Julia's father, Brian, was behind them, and even though he had a tall, wide frame, she could tell he was hiding someone. He stepped to the side, revealing Jessie.

Julia didn't say a word. She and her daughter ran towards each other, exploding into a hug. Julia squeezed tight, sure she was about to wake up from a dream any second.

"You're not supposed to be back for another week!" Julia's voice was muffled against Jessie's denim jacket. "What are you doing here?"

"I changed my flight." Jessie pulled away, her grin beaming from ear to ear. "I couldn't miss your birthday, could I, Mum?"

Julia held Jessie at arm's length. It had only been three weeks since she had driven her to the airport, and yet she looked so different. Her pasty skin had been kissed by the sun, bringing out freckles across her nose and cheeks. Her red-highlighted, dark brown hair had been braided on one side, and she had two piercings in her ear that Julia was sure hadn't been there before.

"I didn't have time to get you anything." Jessie reached into her pocket and pulled out a blue fridge magnet in the shape of Australia. "I grabbed this at the airport."

"It's perfect." Julia fought back the tears as she pulled Jessie into another hug. "I'm so glad you're home. I've missed you so much."

"I missed you too," Jessie whispered, her fingers clinging tightly to Julia. "A lot."

Julia opened her eyes, and through her tears, she saw Billy and Alfie climbing out of Katie's pink Range Rover.

"Hey, Miss S," Billy said, patting her on the shoulder as he walked in. "Happy Birthday."

"Happy Birthday, Julia," Alfie said as he followed him in. "It's good to be home."

Julia finally let go of Jessie when everyone was in the dining room. Mowgli slipped through the crack in Jessie's bedroom door and meowed loudly before circling her feet. She scooped him up and clutched him to her chest.

"What's been going on around here?" Jessie asked as she tickled Mowgli's head. "I feel like I've missed so much."

"The usual," Julia said casually. "This and that."

Jessie raised a sceptical eyebrow raise before shrugging and letting go of Mowgli. They had one last hug before they walked into the dining room to finish the rest of the birthday cake.

Though Julia's life had been flipped upside down recently, as she sat in the dining room with her whole family around her, she felt it flip back to normal. Leah was alive, Brooke and Max were in jail awaiting their trial, and Julia had her daughter back; there was very little else she could wish for on her birthday.

Johnny and Roxy were the first to leave, followed by Katie and Brian, and then Billy and Alfie. Sue and the twins left as the sun started to set, and Dot, as stubborn as usual, stuck around until the last drop of champagne was gone. When Julia, Barker, and Jessie were alone, they exhaled and sat in the familiar silence, glad to be in each other's company.

While Barker showered before bed and Jessie unpacked her suitcase, Julia snuck into her bedroom. She dug to the back of her wardrobe and pulled out a long, plastic, zip-up bag. She hung it on the door and unfastened it to steal another look at her wedding dress. It never failed to make her smile. It was not the tainted dress she had fallen in love with at *Brooke's Bridal Boutique*, but it was a close match, and Julia somehow loved it even more. It had caught her eye when she was walking down Riverswick's high street, and she had instantly known it was the dress for her.

She sat on the edge of the bed and stared at the

dress until she heard the shower cut off. Before Barker could see it, she quickly buried it back in the wardrobe, changed into her pyjamas, and climbed into bed. She snuggled up to Barker when he joined her.

"How was your birthday?" he asked.

"Perfect."

"I suppose you don't want this, then," Barker said, gesturing at himself and raising a cheeky eyebrow.

Julia laughed, brushing a kiss across his lips.

"Perfectly perfect," she whispered, as his mouth once again found hers.

Agatha Frost

## THANK YOU FOR READING &
## DON'T FORGET TO REVIEW!

I hope you all enjoyed venturing into Peridale once again! Writing the journey to Julia and Barker's wedding has been a lot of fun.

If you did enjoy the book, **please consider** writing a review. They help us reach more people! I appreciate any feedback, no matter how long or short. It's a great way of letting other cozy mystery fans know what you thought about the book.

Being an independent author means this is my livelihood, and every review really does make a huge difference. Reviews are the best way to support me so I can continue doing what I love, which is bringing you, the readers, more fun adventures in Peridale! Thank you for spending time in Peridale, and I hope to see you again soon!

ALSO BY AGATHA FROST

If you enjoyed *Champagne and Catastrophes*, why not sign up to Agatha Frost's **FREE** newsletter at **AgathaFrost.com** to hear about brand new releases!

You can also find Agatha on **FACEBOOK**, **TWITTER**, and **INSTAGRAM**. Simply search '**Agatha Frost**'.

**The 15th book in the Peridale Café series is coming soon!** Julia and friends will be back for another Peridale Cafe Mystery case soon.

Made in the USA
Middletown, DE
08 November 2018